# THE WRONG MAN

ADAM CROFT

# GET MORE OF MY BOOKS FREE!

To say thank you for buying this book, I'd like to invite you to my exclusive *VIP Club*, and give you some of my books and short stories for FREE.

To join the club, head to adamcroft.net/vip-club **and two free books will be sent to you straight away! And the best thing is it won't cost you a penny — ever.**

*Adam Croft*

**For more information, visit my website:** adamcroft.net

# BOOKS IN THIS SERIES

Books in the Kempston Hardwick series so far:

To find out more about this series and others, please head to adamcroft.net/list.

*For Deborah Peterson, a great woman and dedicated fan who will be sorely missed.*

1

Kempston Hardwick flicked the beer foam from the arm of his coat and tried to remind himself that the Freemason's Arms was home. As much as he considered anywhere home, that is.

'Sorry mate,' the man in the navy blue boilersuit said, the tone implying that he wasn't particularly sorry at all.

'It's fine. Mistakes happen,' Hardwick replied, his tone implying that mistakes damn well wouldn't happen if people were a little more careful and considerate.

He took a sip of his Campari and orange and swilled it around his mouth. It had been a long time since he'd had one as bad as this. The landlord, Doug Lilley, insisted on bulk-buying ten-litre tubs of almost fluorescent orange 'juice' for use in mixers. Hardwick had often remarked it would be better used to clean the windows, but he couldn't deny it — he quickly got used to it.

That's what he kept telling himself, anyway. That, he maintained, was what kept him coming back here. It certainly wasn't the quality of the drinks or the service, and there was no way it was the cultured, civilised behaviour of the clientele — although the Freemason's Arms was one of the better populated pubs in Tollinghill.

The small market town prided itself on being traditional and upmarket. In reality, it was neither — unless 'traditional' meant backward-thinking and 'upmarket' described the inexplicable house prices.

It was a remarkable town in which to be an observer, though, and Kempston Hardwick was the ultimate observer. Human behaviour had fascinated him for as long as he could remember, and the local pub was — in any town — the melting pot of the local community. No town needed a local newspaper or radio station when it had a place like the Freemason's Arms.

Here, friends and families would gather and pretend to enjoy themselves, all the while repeating the mantra that paying eight pounds for a glass of wine from a bottle that cost three was absolutely fine.

Because this was Tollinghill, home of burying one's head in the sand. Even so, Hardwick much preferred this thin veneer of faux respectability to the out-and-out crassness of many of the surrounding towns.

'Same again?' Doug Lilley, the landlord, asked, sidling over toward Kempston with a glass in his hand.

Hardwick looked down at his own glass, still more than three-quarters full.

'No.'

'Oh well. Suit yourself. Not seen you in here for a while, Kempston.'

'That's because I've not been in here for a while.'

Doug raised an eyebrow. 'Been busy working on your interpersonal skills, I see.'

Hardwick said nothing. He didn't see much point in replying to things which didn't require a reply.

'Here, if you're a fan of whisky you might want to have a drop of this,' the landlord said, handing a presentation cased bottle over the bar to him.

Hardwick looked at the box and could see immediately that this was a pretty special tipple.

'Limited edition, that is. Only ever made a hundred bottles. Forty-six quid for a single measure.'

Hardwick almost choked on his Campari. 'Forty-six pounds? For a sip of whisky?'

'It's good whisky.'

'It'd have to be.'

'You here for the reading?' Doug asked. Hardwick

had seen a couple of posters on the walls of the pub advertising a book launch and reading by local novelist Rupert Pearson.

Although he didn't consider himself a fan of the author, Hardwick had, of course, heard of him. Pearson had won a prestigious national book award a number of years ago, which had catapulted him into the literary limelight. He'd played the 'true to his roots' card ever since and insisted on launching each of his new novels at his local pub, the Freemason's Arms.

'No, just an unfortunate coincidence,' Hardwick replied.

'But you'll stick around for it, though?'

Before Hardwick could even consider his answer, he detected a faint whiff of cheap aftershave and felt the slap of a palm on the back of his shoulder.

'Kempston! Good to see you, mate!'

'Ellis,' Hardwick said, poorly feigning the slightest hint of happiness but not taking his eyes off the bar in front of him.

'How've you been, buddy?'

'Fine, fine.'

It wasn't that Hardwick didn't like Ellis Flint — the man was fairly harmless — it was just that life always had a way of becoming considerably more complicated whenever he appeared in it.

'Been ages since I saw you last!' Ellis said, climbing up onto the stool next to him.

'A fair while, yes.'

'You've been away, someone told me.'

'Here and there.'

'Abroad?'

'Mostly.'

'Wow. I'd love a holiday. Been ages since I've been.'

'Me too.'

'Perhaps we should go away together some time. Again, I mean.'

Hardwick looked at him. 'I don't think that would be wise.'

'I've not been in here much myself, to be honest,' Ellis said, regardless of the fact that Kempston hadn't asked. 'Mrs F's had me on a bit of a diet, see. Said I needed to lose some weight.'

Hardwick looked at Ellis for the first time that night. The man didn't look any different to the last time he saw him. If anything, he'd probably gained a few pounds.

'How long have you been on the diet, Ellis?' Hardwick asked.

'Just over a year now.'

Hardwick nodded. 'Well, you're looking... You're looking happy, Ellis. That's the main thing.'

'Oh, I am. I'm feeling much fitter.'

Hardwick forced a smile. 'Good.'

Doug Lilley took Ellis's order and asked him if he was here for Rupert Pearson's launch.

'Who?' Ellis replied.

'Rupert Pearson. The writer. He has all his launches in here.'

'Never heard of him,' Ellis said. 'And I didn't think you served food.'

'*Launch*, Ellis,' Hardwick said, sighing inwardly. 'His book launch. He's got a new one out, apparently.'

'Ah. Still never heard of him.'

'I think his last book was a good couple of years ago,' Hardwick said.

'That'll be why, then,' said Ellis, who had the memory of a goldfish. 'I don't get much time for reading, that's the thing. Although I've been reading a really good one recently. It's a historical book about this little French bloke living under Roman occupation.'

Hardwick closed his eyes and let out a small sigh. 'Asterix was a Gaul, Ellis.'

'That's what I said. Same thing, ain't it?'

'Try telling the Belgians that.'

Before Ellis could think of something suitable to say in return, they were distracted by one of the pub's regulars, who'd come up to the bar to speak to Doug.

'Seems like there's a bit of a problem,' the man said,

gesturing towards the back room. 'Apparently his publicist hasn't turned up. He says she normally handles all these things.'

Doug shrugged. 'What needs handling? He's done over a dozen of these things here before. She gets up, talks about the book, does a reading from it, sits down and he poses for a few photos. Surely he can manage that on his own?'

'You know more than I do,' the man said. 'The thing he's most bothered about at the moment is that there's no-one to introduce him. Apparently his publicist normally does a talk about the background to the book and all that stuff.'

Doug scratched his bearded chin. 'Right. You wouldn't mind doing that bit would you, Kempston?'

Hardwick looked up, having barely been paying attention up until then. 'Me?'

'Yeah. You're an intelligent bloke. You know about books and stuff.'

'I've only read one Rupert Pearson book, and that was over a decade ago.'

'Exactly. So you know what they're like.'

'I'm pretty sure they're all different. I don't see that me having read and completely forgotten one of his books many years ago qualifies me to talk about his new, different, book.'

'Well, you got any better ideas?' Doug said to Hardwick.

'Yes. He can do it himself. He wrote it.'

The other man shuffled awkwardly. 'I, uh, don't think that's going to cut it. He seems to be pretty super-stitious about stuff like this. He never reads from his own books. If he doesn't have someone else doing the reading, he's not going to come out.'

'Come on, Kempston,' Doug said. 'There's a free drink in it for you.'

Hardwick picked up his glass. 'You should be paying me to drink this as it is.'

Doug raised an eyebrow. 'There are other pubs in Tollinghill. Feel free to go to one of those.'

Ellis Flint leaned in. 'None of them serve Campari though, Kem—'

'Yes, thank you Ellis.' Hardwick glanced towards the back of the pub, across the packed tables of people who'd assembled, waiting for Rupert Person to speak.

'You can get him to sign a copy of his new book for you,' Ellis said.

'Ah. Don't think you will,' Doug interjected. 'He "doesn't do" signings. Says it's wanton destruction of a beautiful work.'

How modest, Hardwick thought. He looked back at

the hopeful faces of Doug Lilley, Ellis Flint and the other man.

'What's the matter, Kempston?' Ellis asked. 'Been tongue-slapped by a fox?'

Hardwick stared at him for a moment, blinking. 'I think the phrase you're looking for is "cat got your tongue", Ellis.'

'Same thing. Point is, Dougie's waiting for an answer.'

Hardwick sighed and closed his eyes. 'Do I have much choice?'

He opened his eyes again to the sight of the three men shaking their heads and smiling.

2

Hardwick held the book in front of him and peered down his not-inconsiderable nose at the text, remembering why he'd never bothered to read a second Rupert Pearson novel.

The crowd watched and waited anxiously, but Kempston Hardwick was not the sort of man to be rushed. Nor would he read something aloud without having first read it to himself.

The room was silent, apart from the occasional tutting or teeth-sucking from Hardwick as he winced his way through the prose.

Eventually, with a slight cough to clear his throat, he began reading.

'The light of the moon fell steadily across the rocks

as Sandra lay her head in his lap, her eyes gazing unwaveringly at the moon. José watched as a lock of hair fell over her face, discarded from her head like,' Hardwick said, pausing. 'Like a disposable coffee cup.

'They could hear the waves lapping at the shore, breaking against the rocks, as if calling them in. Were the night not so chill, they might have been tempted. For now, they watched and waited, caught in a moment from which neither of them wanted to escape. There had been other moments, of course. Other men. But with José she felt comfortable, safe. It was an almost paternal safety, as if José was her father. A father,' he continued, before stopping and clearing his throat again. 'A father with whom she'd quite like to have sex.'

Hardwick looked out at the crowd, and was not altogether surprised to see them enraptured by the reading. If this was how far standards and expectations had fallen, he thought, there really was no hope.

He looked down at the book and continued, unsure as to whether he was more embarrassed for Rupert Pearson or himself.

'"Shall we take a walk?" José said, his accent like butter atop a crumpet. "No," Sandra replied. "I'm content just to lay here, embraced by you."' Hardwick clenched his teeth. Who spoke like that? Not even *he* spoke like that.

'José held her tighter, as if worried the sea foam might take her, dragging her down to the depths of the sea, where the mermaids might claim her as one of their own. And they could. He'd often been struck by how angelic she seemed; how otherworldly. And now, on this night, he truly believed it.'

Kempston closed the book and held it in his hands. He'd promised Rupert Pearson he'd say a few words about the book after reading it, so he did.

'Ladies and gentlemen, that was from The Clarion Call, by Rupert Pearson. Please welcome Rupert Pearson.'

Before even checking to see if the author was on his way to the makeshift stage, Hardwick put the book down and strode back to his bar stool. All of a sudden, another of Doug's Campari and oranges seemed very appetising indeed.

He was already back on his stool before Pearson had realised what was happening and bumbled out from the back room.

'Thank you, thank you ladies and gentlemen,' Pearson said, his gamine smile accepting their applause whilst promising them riches to come.

'I first got the idea for The Clarion Call a number of years ago, and the characters have remained with me ever since, occasionally making themselves known to me once more, yearning for me to write them. Like my very own clarion call, perhaps,' he said, pausing for the rumble of obsequious laughter, which inevitably came.

'I think, in many ways, The Clarion Call is the most difficult novel I've ever written. There's a lot of myself in there. Writing it reminded me of some painful periods in my life, and the book has been a form of therapy for me. And I think that's the real power of literature, isn't it? That it can not just entertain and enthrall the reader, but act as a sort of blood letting for the author. It's a cathartic process at times, and none so much as with this book. Now, I don't want to waffle on too long so I'm going to open the floor to questions. Does anyone have anything they'd like to ask about the book?'

A number of hands shot up. Pearson scanned the room, then pointed towards Hardwick.

'Yes, you there in the denim jacket,' Pearson said, letting Hardwick know that he certainly wasn't talking about him. 'Do you have a question?'

It was Ellis.

'Yes,' Ellis said. 'What's it about?'

A light chuckle rumbled across the room, but Pearson greeted the question with a friendly smile.

'That's a very good question,' he said. 'I guess one might say it's a story of hope. But a sad one, mind. It's a story of someone who's been so badly downtrodden in the past, they see hope and optimism wherever they can, even when that shining light turns out to be nothing more than a dud torch. It's about blind faith, and trying too hard. Sometimes, the best things in life come only when we're not actively seeking them.'

Pearson scanned the room for another raised hand, but was interrupted by Ellis.

'No, I mean what happens? Like, what's it actually about?'

Pearson smiled. 'I think it's a love story.'

'Ah. Doesn't sound like my sort of thing,' Ellis said, perhaps a little too loudly, turning back to the bar and draining half his pint glass into his mouth. He let out a small belch before elbowing Hardwick in the arm. 'So what've you been up to, Kempston? You still living in that spooky church place?'

'The Old Rectory, yes. And there's nothing spooky about it, Ellis.'

'Not now you're down here in the pub, no. But give it a couple of hours…'

'Thank you, Ellis. And to answer your question, I've been travelling. Mostly.'

'Yeah, you said. Whereabouts?'

'A few places. Stockholm. Addis Ababa. Patagonia.'

Ellis nodded slowly, his eyes vacant. 'That in Spain?'

'No, Ellis, it's the southernmost tip of South America. The last land mass before Antarctica, and one of the remotest parts of the world. There's snow in the summer and temperatures can drop to minus twenty when the wind's blowing the wrong way.'

Ellis looked at him. 'Sounds rubbish. Spain's much warmer.'

'Your level of insight knows no bounds, Ellis.'

'Well it's a bit of a weird place to go for a holiday.'

Hardwick took a long sip of his drink. 'It wasn't a holiday.'

Ellis looked at him, quizzical. 'Why did you go there then?'

'I had business to attend to.'

'What, with eskimos?'

'Eskimos are from the arctic and subarctic, Ellis.'

Ellis shuffled slightly in his seat. 'Alright. Well, whoever it is who lives in Patagonia.'

'Patagonians?'

'If you like.'

'I've no particular preference, but I think they'd prefer it.'

'So what's the appeal?' Ellis asked.

Hardwick sat in silence for a few moments, seemingly lost in thought. 'History,' he said, finally.

'What, like fossils and stuff?'

Hardwick nodded slowly. 'Yes. Something like that.'

'Come on, then. Tell me something interesting about the history of Patagonia.'

'I think that would be rather dangerous, Ellis. You've already learned two things today. We wouldn't want to push our luck, would we?'

Ellis nudged Hardwick playfully. 'Ah, come on Kempston. I can never learn too much. I'm like a sponge.'

Hardwick leaned back slightly and looked Ellis up and down. 'Yes,' he said. 'I can see that.'

Ellis just looked at him, his eyes wide open.

'Alright,' Hardwick said, eventually. 'Did you know humans have inhabited Patagonia for thousands upon thousands of years? They've got archaeological findings going back to the thirteenth millennium BC. That's potentially fifteen thousand years ago.'

'Blimey. You'd've thought they'd have gone somewhere warmer by now.'

'Also, the biggest dinosaur ever discovered was found in Patagonia. It weighed seventy-six tons.'

'Crikey,' Ellis said. 'That's nearly as much as Doug.'

'Mmmm?' the landlord said, having appeared, as if by magic, behind the pair.

'Nothing,' Ellis said, quickly.

'You both enjoying the evening then, lads?' Doug said, placing a hand on each of their shoulders.

Hardwick forced a less than convincing smile. 'Indeed.'

3

Hardwick wasn't the sort of person who tended to get hangovers, but he had to admit his head felt a little fuzzy as he was woken the next morning by the ringing of his phone.

There were times — not often — when he wished he had a mobile phone. But that was usually only when he was forced to make his way downstairs and into his living room to answer the vintage GPO bakelite phone on his side table.

'Hardwick,' he said, placing the receiver to his ear.

'Kempston. It's Doug, from the Freemason's.'

'Oh. Morning Doug,' Hardwick said, desperately trying to remember what he'd done last night. He was fairly sure he hadn't caused any trouble. Ellis, on the other hand, he couldn't vouch for. Nor was he the man's keeper.

'Just wondered if you'd heard the news.'

Hardwick let this hang in the air for a few moments. 'Sorry, Doug. You're going to need to be a little more specific than that.'

'That's a no, then,' Doug said. Hardwick could almost hear the awkward shuffle at the other end of the line. 'You remember last night, Rupert Pearson was stressing because his PA hadn't turned up? Well, she was found dead in the early hours of the morning.'

'Dead?'

'Murdered, according to the police. They were round here first thing, asking questions. It had been in her diary that she was spending the evening in the pub doing this bloody book launch for Pearson.'

Hardwick squeezed his eyes shut and tried to force the headache away. 'What makes them think she was murdered?'

'That's what I said. Apparently she was beaten pretty badly. She was found up at Tollinghill Country Park. By a dog walker, believe it or not.'

He could. It was an old cliché that it was usually dog walkers who found dead bodies, but it was often true. After all, many killers tended to try to hide their victims' bodies — usually in woods or undergrowth — and these were exactly the sorts of places dog walkers went in the dawn hours.

'I see,' Hardwick said, unsure what else to add. 'Do they know when she died?'

'I overheard that DI Warner bloke saying she was killed at ten past nine yesterday evening.'

'That's remarkably precise,' Hardwick replied.

'Yeah. Apparently the pathologist only narrowed it down to an hour or two, but then Warner noticed her watch had been smashed and broken in the attack, and had stopped at ten past nine. Bit of a giveaway, that.'

'Well yes, it is rather.'

'Sad, too, to think she was still alive while we were all stressing about the fact she hadn't turned up. You were probably in the middle of doing your introductory bit while the poor girl was being bludgeoned to death.'

'Well yes, I suppose so,' Hardwick said.

'Gets you off the hook at least,' Doug added, his throaty laugh announcing years of cigarette smoking. 'But get this. They've already made an arrest. Quick or what?'

'Impressive,' Hardwick said, unsure exactly what he was supposed to gain from this conversation.

'One of my locals. Bloke by the name of Terry Cox. You know him.'

'I don't,' Hardwick replied.

'Yeah you do. Terry. You know Terry.'

'Trust me, I don't know anybody called Terry.'

'Yeah you do. He's in here all the time.'

Hardwick sighed slightly. 'He may well be, but I'm not.'

'Terry and Veronica have been knocking around together recently. Past few months, anyway. They've mostly been over at the King's Arms. It's closer to her house.'

'If he's not been in your pub and I've not been in your pub, how do you expect me to know him?' Hardwick asked.

'He was in here yesterday afternoon. With her. Had a right old barney, they did. You must remember.'

Hardwick thought back to yesterday afternoon, when he'd first gone into the Freemason's Arms. He recalled a couple arguing in the street outside the pub as he went in, but hadn't seen them come out of the Freemason's. Was this the couple Doug was referring to?

'Quite a small chap, is he? Shaved head, bomber jacket?'

'Yeah, that's Terry.'

'And she had long, slightly curly ginger hair, taller than him, smartly dressed, Michael Kors handbag, mole on her left cheek?'

'Got a much better look at her than you did at him, didn't you?'

'There was more to look at.'

'You're telling me.'

'No, I mean she had more distingui—'

'But anyway, I thought you might like to know,' Doug said, interrupting him.

Hardwick raised his eyebrows slightly, as if Doug could actually see him over the phone. 'I see. Pray tell why?'

'Well, you like murder and stuff don't you? Figured it was your sort of bag.'

Doug's comment struck Hardwick as both accurate and wildly inaccurate at the same time. It was true to say he had assisted in a few murderers being brought to justice over the past handful of years, and had grudgingly accepted Ellis's help in doing so.

It had all started with the death of a stand-up comedian in the Freemason's Arms a few years earlier. He and Ellis had solved the murder and helped bring the killer to justice, despite Detective Inspector Rob Warner having Hardwick thrown in a cell for interfering in his investigation.

All in all, he'd caught four killers — all despite the ineptitude of the local constabulary on three occasions, and the Greek police on another. He couldn't even have a holiday without having to solve a murder.

He had, on more than one occasion, wondered if Ellis Flint was some sort of curse on him. Whenever Ellis popped up, there was a dead body and a murder to be solved. There was never any suspicion that Ellis might be responsible — the man couldn't even tie his own shoelaces — but every time he met the man he secretly wondered if this might be his last day on Earth.

It was something that often made him feel uneasy, as well it might. But right now there was something else niggling away at him; a thought he couldn't quite put his finger on, but which deeply troubled him.

4

The fresh air went some way towards clearing the last of Hardwick's hangover as he walked through the centre of Tollinghill on his journey from the Old Rectory to the Freemason's Arms.

He hadn't been drinking much recently, and the previous day's brief afternoon had turned into a long night. That tended to happen when Ellis Flint was around, and mere hours later he found himself heading back to the Freemason's, where he'd arranged to meet Ellis.

A thought had been troubling him ever since he'd received the call from Doug earlier that day. A thought he couldn't quite shake from his mind.

'Your seat's still warm, Kempston,' Ellis said, chuckling to himself as Hardwick entered the pub.

Hardwick barely noticed the comment, tied up as he was in his own thoughts.

'The usual?' Doug Lilley asked.

'Uh, no,' Hardwick replied. 'I think I'll have a coffee.'

'Don't think you will. We don't do coffee.'

Hardwick looked at the landlord for a moment. 'Right. What have you got?'

'Got a coffee porter on here,' Doug replied, locking his fingers round one of the handpulls. 'Only five percent.'

'Five percent what?' Hardwick asked, raising an eyebrow.

'Alcohol.'

'I know. I was trying to make a... Actually, don't worry. I'll have a half of that, then. If nothing else, it might help as hair of the dog.'

'You sure you don't want to try that limited edition whisky?' Doug asked.

'Not at forty-six pounds a go, I don't,'

'You get home alright last night, Kempston?' Ellis asked, before taking a sip of his own beer.

'No, Ellis. I died.'

'Oh well. Can't beat bad luck, can you?'

'We'll have no more deaths around here, thank you

very much,' Doug said, plonking a full pint of dark beer in front of Kempston.

'I asked for a half,' Hardwick said, looking at the landlord.

'My hand slipped. Three eighty, please.'

Hardwick handed over his money and tried to divert conversation towards the matter in hand.

'Veronica Campbell,' Doug said over his shoulder, whilst putting the money in the till. 'That was her name.'

It was as if Doug could read Hardwick's mind. 'And she was the woman who was arguing outside the pub when I came in yesterday?'

'Quite possibly. Sounds like her, anyway. And the way you described Terry on the phone definitely sounds like him. Weird bloke.'

'Weird, but not a murderer?' Hardwick asked.

Doug smiled at him. 'You took the words right out of my mouth.'

'What is it, Kempston?' Ellis asked. 'Don't you think it was him?'

Hardwick took a deep breath, then sighed. 'I don't know. I don't have any of the facts, and I've never spoken to either of them. All I do know is I've looked into the eyes of many murderers in my life. There's something there. Something I can't describe, and can't quite put my finger on. It's almost like a dull sparkle. Just... something. When I crossed the road to come in here last night, I made eye contact with him. I vaguely recognised him, perhaps from in here. I could tell they were arguing, and we held eyes for a second or two, maybe more. Call me mad for having nothing but a hunch, but if you ask me, I didn't look into the eyes of a murderer.'

There was silence for a few moments before Ellis spoke.

'I don't know why they don't just do away with all the major crime teams and just get you to go around looking in people's eyes, Kempston.'

'Don't be facetious,' Hardwick replied. 'I told you it was only a hunch. But, more often than not, my hunches turn out to be correct.'

'He's right,' Doug said, nodding slowly. 'I know Terry. He drinks in here quite a bit. Or did until he met that Veronica bird. Don't get me wrong, he's a nasty piece of work. He deserves to go down for something, alright. You should see the way he talks to people. The way he treated her. The way he spoke to her yesterday.'

'Did you hear what they were arguing about?' Hardwick asked.

'Bits and bobs. I don't know what sparked it off. They were sitting over there by the fire. Wasn't particularly busy yesterday afternoon, and I could see the conversation getting a bit more animated. I could tell from the body language they weren't exactly whispering sweet nothings into each other's ears. Then they got a bit louder and she mentioned something about one of them having to do something to earn some money. Sounded to me like she was having a go at him for not working and just wanting to go out drinking all the time. She'd probably mentioned she was going to have to go home and get ready for the launch in the evening. Knowing Terry, he probably told her to sack it off and stay out drinking.'

'And that's what it was all over?' Hardwick asked.

Doug shrugged. 'I dunno. Like I say, I don't know how it started, but that's when it started getting loud enough for me to hear. Next thing I know, he's calling her a selfish bitch, telling her he doesn't know why he bothers trying to spend time with her. All that sort of stuff. They'd both had a couple of drinks by then, so it didn't take much to get the fire going.'

'And she was planning to work that evening?'

'Well, if you call it work. She only had to introduce old Rupert whatsisface and blab on about how brilliant his new book is. People are always drinking at these things. It's not exactly a corporate board meeting, is it?'

'No, I suppose not,' Hardwick said, feeling the last remnants of his headache disappearing.

'But if you ask me, it's no bad thing Terry being

locked up. He deserves to go down for something. It's about time he got what was coming to him.'

'Not a popular chap, then?' Hardwick asked.

'You could say that. He could start a fight in an empty room, Terry.'

'That's as may be, but it doesn't mean it's right that he goes down for murder.'

'No, but if he didn't do it they won't send him down will they?'

Hardwick wished this were true. He'd seen far too many injustices in his time to know that the police didn't always get it right. Far from it, when it came to the local police force in Tollinghill.

And injustices weren't something Hardwick could stand. He'd seen first-hand how they could ruin lives and blight whole families. It wasn't something he could ever stand by and let happen, no matter how much he had to put his own life on the line.

What he needed was more information. Something that could tell him about the background to Veronica Campbell's death.

'Where does Rupert Pearson live, exactly?' Hardwick asked Doug.

'Out on the Shafford road, just past the old petrol station before you leave town. You can't miss it. It's the only one up there. Big black gates at the front.'

Hardwick nodded slowly. 'Ellis, drink up. We're going to go and have a word with somebody.'

'Who?' Ellis asked, grabbing his glass and gulping down three mouthfuls.

'The person who perhaps knew Veronica Campbell best, Ellis. We're going to see Rupert Pearson.'

5

The walk from the Freemason's Arms to Rupert Pearson's house took far longer than Ellis Flint thought it had any right to. Then again, Ellis Flint wasn't one for walking at the best of times.

The road heading north out of Tollinghill seemed fairly steep in the car, but it was practically Himalayan on foot.

Ellis huffed and puffed as Hardwick explained a little about what he knew about Pearson.

'To all intents and purposes, he's been pretty successful, Ellis. He's about the only one of the so-called "literary" writers who's been able to sustain a regular output of work over the past few years. Although, of course, I take issue with the term "literary". It's snobbery at the best of times, but verging on the ridiculous when referring to the sort of tripe Rupert Pearson produces.'

Ellis didn't know whether to be more surprised at Kempston Hardwick calling someone else a snob, or the fact that the man could march at this speed and still manage to string a sentence together without sounding even slightly out of breath.

'Yeah?' he puffed, realising that Mrs F's diet hadn't exactly improved his fitness.

'Would you believe, Ellis, there's even talk that he'll be knighted in the next New Year's Honours list? Can you imagine? Sir Rupert Pearson. For services to literature, no less! It makes a mockery of the whole system, if you ask me. But then again the British public have never exactly been prime arbiters of what constitutes good taste.'

'No,' Ellis said — just about.

'So, let's make sure we're clear on everything before we get there. Veronica Campbell dies at 9.10pm, yes?' Hardwick didn't wait for Ellis to reply. 'We can then discount everyone who was in the Freemason's Arms, as you and I both know those people to have somewhere close to a hundred alibis. Terry Cox, of course, is not one of those. Fifteen love to DI Warner. But that doesn't mean Cox is guilty. Presumably the eminent Detective Inspector has more to go on than that, but we shall cross that bridge when we come to it. Personally, it seems to me as though there's something sitting just under the surface which needs uncovering. Something I can almost see, and which doesn't feel quite... Yes. Interesting.'

'Yeah?' Ellis puffed, noticing Hardwick had stopped walking.

'Mmmm.'

Ellis took a few seconds to try and get his breath back before speaking. 'Why've you stopped?' he said, eventually.

Hardwick looked at him blankly. 'Because we're here, Ellis.'

'Shall we walk up the drive then?' Ellis asked, his eyes narrowed.

'Indeed. Let's.'

The driveway was long and gravelled, but not at all level. It had clearly been a while since it'd had much attention, the potholes still full of water from the last rainfall three days earlier.

From the driveway one could, if one wanted, walk all the way around the house and into the back garden. The house — a tall, impressive-looking Georgian building — appeared to have been plonked in the middle of the land, with no real boundaries or indication as to where the front garden ended and the back began. Hardwick supposed that, with the front gates shut, the whole area would be kept pretty private.

Hardwick rang the doorbell and the pair waited for signs of life. A few moments later, they heard the sound of a key rattling in the door, which opened to reveal the familiar figure of Rupert Pearson.

'Mr Pearson, Kempston Hardwick. We met last night at the Freemason's Arms.'

'Oh. Yes. The chap who did the introduction. I'm terribly sorry, but I'm afraid I've just had some dreadful news. Is it possible I could call you another time?'

'I know,' Hardwick said. 'In fact, that's why we've come to see you.'

Pearson cocked his head to the side slightly, then stood aside. 'Oh. Well, in that case you'd better come in.'

Hardwick very much liked the inside of Rupert Pearson's house. Pearson was clearly a man of good taste, regardless of how insufferable Hardwick found his books.

'Molière,' Hardwick remarked, gesturing towards a

collection of works on the bookcase in the hallway. 'And in the original French, too.'

'Don't speak a word,' Pearson said, forcing a smile. 'First editions, though. Got to keep the most impressive ones on display downstairs. I keep my Mills and Boon upstairs.'

Hardwick let out a small chuckle, startling Ellis Flint for a moment. He wasn't entirely sure he'd ever seen Hardwick laugh.

'"Some of the most famous books are the least worth reading. Their fame was due to their having done something that needed to be doing in their day. The work is done and the virtue of the book has expired,"' Hardwick said, quoting Molière himself.

Pearson smiled. 'Never read them in English either.'

'The great man would have approved,' Hardwick said. '"I live on good soup, not on fine words."'

'What's soup got to do with it?' Ellis asked, frowning.

'It's a quote, Ellis. It means... Actually, let's not worry too much about that, shall we?'

'Tea? Coffee?' Pearson asked, leading the pair through into his not inconsiderable kitchen.

'Tea, thank you,' Hardwick said. 'No milk, no sugar.'

Pearson looked at Ellis. 'Same for you...?'

'Oh, sorry,' Ellis replied, walking over and offering his hand. 'Ellis Flint. I'm a friend of Kempston's.'

'Nice to meet you, Ellis. Milk?'

'Please.'

'Sugar?'

'Four please.'

Hardwick raised an eyebrow at him.

'Actually, make that three.'

Hardwick rolled his eyes and sat down at the kitchen table.

'Mr Pearson, we're very sorry to hear about what happened to Veronica. It's a shame we never got to meet her.'

Pearson, who was busy spooning copious amounts of sugar into a mug, stopped moving, his back to Hardwick and Flint as he paused for a moment. 'It is. It's a huge shame. She was a marvellous woman. Oh, don't get me wrong, she had her demons. Don't we all? But she was an absolute genius at her job. I really have no idea what I'm going to do without her.' Pearson was visibly shaken. 'Sorry,' he said, sitting down. 'You said you wanted to speak to me about Veronica.'

'Yes, that's right,' Hardwick said. 'I understand she was supposed to be at the Freemason's Arms last night?'

'Yes. She organises all these sorts of things. Launches, events, engagements. She usually does a sort of introduction, reads a bit from the book and then I come on and do a short speech and answer questions.'

'Do you not do your own readings?' Hardwick asked.

'Oh no. I think it's dreadfully vain when authors do that. Books, for me, have very clearly defined lineations. Authors write them, readers read them. Anything else is just crass.'

Hardwick didn't disagree with the man's views, but he was more struck by the way in which he spoke. This was clearly a man who was well educated and who chose his words carefully. It was just a shame he had to lower his standards for the purpose of his readers.

'And all of your launches happen at the Freemason's Arms?' Hardwick asked.

'Yes, pretty much. It's something I like to do. I'm not fond of the big London launches or anything like that. I prefer to keep it friendly and local. I've got quite a big readership round here. I like it that way.'

'Do you not like doing events and things then?' Ellis asked, slurping at his tea.

'Not especially. It's not my sort of thing. Sorry, were you friends of Veronica's or...?'

'Sort of,' Hardwick said. 'In a manner of speaking. What time was she meant to be at the Freemason's Arms last night?'

'She'd usually arrive around eight o'clock for a start

at nine. There's not a whole lot to do, really. Rearranging tables and chairs, mostly. Sometimes there's a press element, but that's rare nowadays. Once you've done one book launch you've done them all. Plus it's nigh-on impossible to get a journalist or photographer on the local rag to work much beyond three in the afternoon. I got there about quarter past eight, and I think I probably started to get worried at about half past. She was never usually one for being late, but just recently she'd been a little tardier than usual, so I half expected she might be running slightly behind. By the time it got closer to nine o'clock I began to panic and and was wondering why she hadn't turned up.'

'The police say she was still alive at that point,' Hardwick said. 'She was... Her watch was broken in the attack. It showed the time as ten past nine. The pathologist agreed that was about right for the time of death, based on... Well, you know.'

'I do. And I wish I didn't,' Pearson said quietly.

Ellis Flint shuffled uncomfortably in his chair. He never felt quite right whenever Hardwick went around interviewing people. He had an odd way of putting people at ease without actually saying anything. Perhaps it was his aura of authority. In any case, very rarely did anyone challenge him or enquire as to why he was asking such personal questions. Indeed, many assumed he was a police officer — something he'd never been and never would be.

'You mentioned she was a little more... relaxed, recently?' Hardwick asked casually, sipping his tea.

'Yes. She's always been an absolute powerhouse. An extraordinary woman. A superb PA and a PR genius. She organised absolutely everything. She was the real force behind the Rupert Pearson brand. A few months back she started seeing this fellow. Terry something or other. Bit of a local thug, by all accounts. Christ knows what she saw in him. Probably the attraction of danger. That's what they reckon women like, isn't it? Can't quite see the appeal myself. But anyway, she'd been seeing a lot of him and had been drinking more heavily. She and her husband got divorced about eighteen months back. She kept the house — one of those cottages on Park Road — and her husband, David, ended up buying a place on Laurel Street, down by the doctor's surgery. I think it was something that gradually progressed from there. She was... more irritable, I suppose I'd call it. Short-tempered. It was as if the schedule and routine had gone out of her life. She needed structure.'

'What are your views on Terry?' Hardwick asked.

Pearson lifted his eyebrows and shook his head slowly. 'I don't have any. I never actually met him. She mentioned to me she was seeing someone called Terry, and somebody mentioned something to me in town a couple of months back about Veronica being seen out with a chap who had a bit of a reputation.'

Hardwick nodded. 'Did it affect her work at all?'

'No, not really. That's the strange thing about it. I mean, the job's not one where she needed to work set hours. There was plenty that needed to be done, but whether she wanted to do it at midday or three o'clock in the morning made absolutely no difference to me. It was only when it came to things like launches and interviews where she'd turn up late — or not at all, in the case of last night.'

'I think she had a pretty good excuse last night,' Ellis said.

'If it was past nine o'clock when she died, she was still alive when she was meant to be at the Freemason's Arms. Perhaps if she'd been a little more professional and actually turned up when she... I'm sorry,' Pearson said, composing himself. 'It's all terribly distressing. Veronica worked with me for fifteen years. I'd never dreamed of working with anyone else. But now...'

For Hardwick, the contrast was extraordinary. The Rupert Pearson he'd met the previous night had been confident, assured and in control. Now, though, he seemed like a man who didn't know which way to turn.

6

'Thoughts?' Ellis asked as the pair made their way back down the hill from Rupert Pearson's house, the pace somewhat slower this time.

Hardwick raised an eyebrow. 'That's never a wise question to ask someone like me, Ellis.'

'Alright. I'll tell you what I think then,' Ellis replied, not surprising Hardwick in the slightest. 'Rupert Pearson knew Veronica pretty well, right? They'd worked together for years. If he'd spotted a big change in her after meeting this Terry bloke, I think it's fair to say Terry had influence over her. Some sort of power, perhaps. Rupert said himself that Veronica was organised, outgoing and all the rest of it. When two people like that collide, well... It's a recipe for disaster, isn't it?'

'You still think Terry Cox killed her, don't you?' Hardwick said, with a tone of voice which sounded as though he was accusing Ellis of thinking the Earth was flat.

'I'm just saying it's the most likely possibility. We've heard what he was like. He's the only person who knew Veronica on any great level who could have actually killed her, because everyone else was at the book launch. And most murders are committed by someone close to the victim, right?'

'Correct. *Most* murders. Not all.'

'Yes, but it holds a lot more water than "I looked into his eyes and he seemed alright". I can't imagine that one going down all that well in court.'

'Which is why we need more evidence, Ellis. I'm well aware my hunch doesn't count as evidence, but it's a starting point. It'll set us off in the right direction.'

'You hope.'

Hardwick stopped walking and turned towards him. 'When have I ever been wrong in the past, Ellis?'

'Lots of times. There was the time when you—'

'Yes, but the hunch is always correct. When I suspect something is amiss, I'm usually right. There are always hiccups and stumbling blocks along the way, but we're dealing with killers here, Ellis. Clever people. Not to mention the deliberate obstructions caused by stupid people too.'

'DI Warner?' Ellis asked.

'I wouldn't be so crass as to label a ranked officer of Her Majesty's police force in such a way, but at the same time I shan't correct you unnecessarily.'

'Which is your way of saying you think he's a bit of a plonker.'

'Is that a statement or a question, Ellis?'

'It's a statement.'

'Then it doesn't require a response from me,' he said, and continued walking.

Ellis fought to catch up.

'So what now? I suppose you're going to carry on with this fantasy in your head that there's another evil genius living somewhere in Tollinghill, rubbing their hands at the thought of having got away with yet another heinous murder?'

'Someone's been reading the dictionary,' Hardwick said.

'What's next, Kempston? Are you going to march into the police station and demand to see their internal files or break into the dead woman's house and rummage through her cutlery drawer?'

'Neither,' Hardwick replied. 'I will indeed visit Miss Campbell's property in the course of fleshing out the information I have available to me, but first of all I'm going to visit Detective Inspector Warner and *ask* to see his internal files.'

Ellis laughed. 'And when he tells you to naff off?'

'I'll show him these,' Hardwick said, producing a brown envelope from his jacket pocket with a flourish.

'What is it?'

'It's an envelope, Ellis.'

'I know, but what's inside it?'

'Open it and find out.'

Ellis, after pausing for a moment, did as he was told. His eyes opened wide, his jaw dropping as he registered the subject matter of the photos inside the envelope.

'Jesus Christ, Kempston! Where did you get these?'

'A mutual friend.'

'Christ. Well, I do apologise. I was wrong. You're not going to make rude demands of the police after all. You're just going to blackmail them.'

'It's not blackmail, Ellis. It's a friendly nudge to let Detective Inspector Warner know that I too have information which I've been cautious not to share. It's nothing more than a business deal.'

'Well I've got to hand it to you, Kempston. Just when I think you can't surprise me any more, you go and drop something like that.'

'If it results in us identifying and catching a killer, Ellis, I think you'll agree it's all perfectly reasonable.'

Ellis nodded slowly. 'Yes. Yes, I can see the logic. But I do have just one question.'

'Go on,' Hardwick said, not slowing.

'What's that?' he asked, pointing to a dark corner of one of the photos.

'I believe they're what's known as crotchless panties, Ellis.'

Ellis blinked rapidly, then nodded his head awkwardly and handed the envelope back to Hardwick.

7

Kempston Hardwick was no stranger to Tollinghill Police Station. Not only had he visited on a number of occasions to speak to Detective Inspector Rob Warner about ongoing murder cases (or 'interfering' as Warner liked to put it) but he'd even spent a few hours in a cell a few years back for asking one too many questions (or 'breaking and entering' as Warner had put it).

Hardwick could see fear in the civilian receptionist's eyes as he approached the front desk.

'Ah, hello. May I speak to Detective Inspector Rob Warner, please?'

'Uh, can I ask who wants to see him and what it's about, please?' the young woman asked.

'You know very well who wants to see him, because I could see the colour drain from your face the moment I walked in. And as for the purpose of my visit, I'm afraid I can't divulge that information.'

The receptionist tried to regain the upper ground. 'I'm still going to need some identification, sir, and at least a brief summary of what you want to see DI Warner about.'

'It's classified police business,' Hardwick replied.

'Then you can tell me, seeing as I'm police staff. And you're not.'

Hardwick smiled. 'Then you do know who I am, and the first part of your question is answered. As for the second, you may let Detective Inspector Warner know it concerns the death of Miss Veronica Campbell.'

The receptionist nodded her head in a way which told Kempston she had fully expected him to say that, and explained that she'd try to call DI Warner's office but couldn't guarantee he'd even be in, never mind available to see him.

'Oh, he's definitely in. His car's in the car park,' Kempston said. 'Dark green Vauxhall Astra, registration Foxtrot Oscar Zero Seven Hotel Lima Mike. MOT'd in June, road fund licence expires next Thursday. Cutting it fine. I'll mention it to him.'

'He might be in a meeting,' the receptionist said, meekly.

'In which case we'll be only too happy to wait, won't

we Ellis?' he said, not giving Ellis a chance to reply. 'Does the vending machine still get stuck if you order Minstrels?'

The receptionist blinked a few times. 'Uh, it does, but it's not too bad if you give it a whack while the thing's turning.'

'Thank you. Over here alright?' he said, pointing to two chairs, which were bolted to the wall.

The receptionist smiled and nodded slowly, before picking up the phone. Hardwick couldn't hear the conversation, but a few seconds later she put the phone back down and called across to him.

'Detective Inspector Warner says he's extremely busy, but if you can leave him a note he'll take a look and get back to you.'

'In which case, could you give him a call back and tell him Bubbles sent me?'

The receptionist cocked her head slightly. Hardwick smiled and nodded.

She picked up the phone and mumbled something inaudible into the mouthpiece. After a momentary pause, she repeated the last word, as if Warner hadn't quite heard her properly. Hardwick watched her mouth as she said the word 'Bubbles', followed by a surprised look on her face as Warner slammed the phone down at the other end.

'Uh, I can't say for certain,' she said, calling across again, 'but I think he might be on his way down. Who's Bubbles?'

Before Hardwick could answer, a door flew open and a pale Detective Inspector Warner marched over and shook Hardwick's and Flint's hands, before ushering them through the door he'd just come in from.

'Hello, gentlemen. Apologies for that — lots going on at the moment, but I'm sure I can find some time for you. Do come this way, won't you?'

Warner led the pair down a corridor and into a side room. He flicked a switch and an overhead light hummed before finally kicking into action.

'Right, what's this all about?' he said, as the door closed behind them.

'Shall we take a seat?' Hardwick said.

Warner shuffled his feet and nodded, before gesturing to the table and chairs which had been placed up against the wall. It seemed to Hardwick as though this was an informal and rarely-used interview room.

'It's about the murder of Veronica Campbell,' Hardwick said. 'I believe you have someone in custody.'

'Do you? I couldn't possibly say. We haven't released any details to the media yet.'

'Oh come on, Detective Inspector. Not only is it the

twenty-first century, but this is Tollinghill. A branch of Poundland would last longer in this place than a secret.'

'Why are you here, Hardwick?' Warner asked. 'No, wait. Let me guess. We've got the wrong man and you think there's a masked killer lurking the streets and ducking down dark alleys every time a police car drives past.'

'He saw it in his eyes,' Ellis added, helpfully.

'In his eyes?' Warner said. 'Here we go.'

'I think you've got the wrong man, yes,' Hardwick replied.

'On what grounds?'

'On which grounds have you arrested him, Detective Inspector?'

'Are you his lawyer?'

'Of course not.'

'Then we're not at liberty to discuss that sort of information with a member of the public,' Warner said, almost spitting out the last few words.

'Alright. Let's have a look at the indisputable facts. You arrested Terry Cox pretty quickly after Veronica Campbell was found dead. Has Terry Cox been charged?'

'Like I said, we haven't named anybody yet.'

'Okay. Has anyone been charged with the murder of Veronica Campbell?'

'Murder investigations are complicated, Mr Hardwick. These things take time.'

'Has anyone been charged, Detective Inspector?'

Warner sighed. 'Not yet, no.'

'Right. We're now, what, fourteen, fifteen hours on from Terry Cox's arrest? Yet either the Crown Prosecution Service haven't authorised a charge or you haven't gathered enough evidence to feel confident in going for a charge.'

'It's a murder case, Hardwick. We need to get it right.'

'Fifteen hours is a lot of time to get it right. Especially when it comes to unplanned murder committed in a fit of rage or passion. You and I both know that.'

'With all due respect, I think I know a bit more about it than you do,' Warner said.

'She was beaten to death in the middle of the country park and crudely hidden in the undergrowth. Her attacker would be covered in blood. There'd be DNA everywhere. You arrested Cox within hours of her death, in which case he'd have traces of her blood and DNA all over him. Even if he'd been in the shower since, there's no way he'd get it all off. And his clothes would be covered. They'd have left traces all over his house. By now, you'd have all that evidence to hand and would be pushing for a charge. If you had it, that is. If it existed, you'd have it. But you don't. Therefore it can't exist. Therefore, Terry Cox didn't kill Veronica Campbell.'

Warner folded his arms and looked at Hardwick. 'You think you're so bloody clever, don't you?'

'I'm not actually in need of positive reinforcement at the moment, Detective Inspector Warner, but I appreciate the sentiment. Thank you for your kind words.'

'Hardwick, if you think you're going to interfere in another bloody investigation of mine, you can think again. I'm not afraid to have you banged up again, you know.'

'Nor am I afraid to spend a night in the cells, Detective Inspector, although it was a little cold last time. Left me with terrible cramp. Do you happen to know anyone who dabbles in a little massage?'

Hardwick noticed Warner's face flush red.

Ellis, who'd not said a word the whole time they'd been in the police station, was quite enjoying watching Hardwick tie Warner in knots.

'Alternatively, of course,' Hardwick said, continuing, 'I find the occasional reveal of helpful information tends to warm my blood enough to stave off the pain.'

'You know I can't share sensitive information,' Warner said, shuffling uncomfortably.

Hardwick smiled and stood. 'It needn't be sensitive,

Detective Inspector. I'll call you if I need to ask anything. I really do appreciate your help.'

Hardwick opened the door and marched back down the corridor, Ellis following behind him.

'Very enlightening, thank you!' Hardwick called to the receptionist, who didn't have time to respond before they were back out on the high street.

'Wait up, Kempston,' Ellis said, puffing. 'If you've got Warner's phone number, why didn't you just phone him in the first place?'

'Well, they're terribly impersonal things, phone calls, aren't they? Besides which, you can't watch someone squirm over the phone.'

8

To Ellis, Hardwick seemed like a man energised by his recent battle of wits with DI Warner. He'd seen Hardwick at his best on many occasions, but he still managed to throw a curveball every time which left Ellis open-mouthed.

They'd barely got twenty yards from the police station before Hardwick stopped suddenly, raised a hand in the air and turned around, before crossing the road and ducking down a side street.

'Where are we going, Kempston?'

'To see Veronica's ex-husband, Ellis, get a bit of background colour.'

'But we don't know where he lives,' Ellis said, jogging to keep up with him.

'We know he lives on Laurel Street. Rupert Pearson said so.'

'Laurel Street's massive! It goes on for a good mile or two.'

'Four hundred and twenty five yards, Ellis. Don't exaggerate. In any case, Pearson told us he lives near the doctor's surgery. Pretty handy, actually.'

'Handy?' Ellis asked. 'Why?'

Ellis's question was answered when they reached the doctor's surgery and Hardwick walked inside. He waited patiently in line at the reception desk while Ellis tugged at his sleeve, before it was his turn to be seen.

'Hello. My name's David Campbell. I moved house recently but can't remember if I changed my address with you or not. It should be Laurel Street.'

'Okay, one moment,' the receptionist said, tapping at her computer. 'Ah yes, here we go. Number ninety-six?'

'That's the one,' Hardwick said. 'I did change it after all. Not to worry. Thank you.'

Hardwick turned and walked out, leaving Ellis standing in front of the reception desk.

The receptionist smiled sweetly at him, as if expecting him to speak. 'Oh. Sorry. Are you together?'

'Yes. Sorry. Well, no. Not together together. Not like that. He's a friend. Just a friend. Good old David.' Ellis chuckled nervously, before turning and following Hardwick.

By the time he'd got outside, Hardwick had already crossed the street and was making his way towards number 96.

'That was a bit risky, wasn't it?' he said, when he finally caught up with him.

'Not in the slightest. The majority of Tollinghill's registered at that surgery — particularly those who live in the same street.'

'No, but what if she'd challenged you and asked you to confirm your whole address or something?'

'Why would she? I gave a full name and a street. More than enough to satisfy any suspicions. Anyway Ellis, it's a matter of confidence. If you go in biting your fingernails and looking like you're about to commit armed robbery they'll see right through you. People pick up on things like that. It's an almost animalistic— Ah, here we are. Number ninety-six.'

Before Ellis could say anything, Hardwick knocked on the door.

A few moments later, Ellis saw a dark figure moving towards them through the frosted glass. The door opened.

'Mr Campbell?' Hardwick said. 'Sorry to disturb

you. My name's DI Kempston Hardwick, and this is my colleague Ellis Flint. May we come in?'

Ellis smiled and tried not to roll his eyes. The assumption, of course, was that David Campbell would believe that DI stood for Detective Inspector and not Hardwick's first two names — Dagwood Isambard. He'd remarked to Ellis in the past that he felt Kempston was the least egregious of the three names he'd been given.

'Yes, of course,' Campbell said, ushering them inside. 'I presume it's about Veronica?'

'It is,' Hardwick said, admiring the long, Edwardian-style hallway in Campbell's otherwise modest home.

'Two of your colleagues came to visit me this morning. Massive shock, I've got to say.'

'Yes, it must be a very upsetting time for you. Did you have children together, may I ask?'

'No, fortunately not. For many reasons.'

'How do you mean?' Hardwick asked.

'Well, a divorce and a death inside two years is a lot for anyone to handle, without it affecting children at the same time.'

'Yes, I suppose it must be.'

'Sorry,' Campbell said, realising the three were still standing in the hall. 'Come on through to the kitchen. Tea? Coffee?'

'We're fine, thank you,' Hardwick said, a hand on Ellis's arm as he watched David Campbell enter the kitchen. 'Wouldn't want you getting another sugar rush, Ellis.'

The pair joined David in the kitchen and sat down at the wooden table.

'I understand you've not been here long,' Hardwick said.

'That's right. Veronica got the house after we divorced, and I moved into rented before coming here a few months ago after everything was finalised.'

'That's remarkably generous of you.'

David chuckled. 'You say that, but in reality I couldn't stand the place. It's one of the cottages up Park Road. You know, the ones with the thatched roofs. Not my sort of thing at all. All oak beams and wonky walls. But Veronica loved it.'

'Which number Park Road?' Hardwick asked.

'Number fourteen. I mentioned it to your colleagues earlier. Do you not have it on record?'

'We've been out all morning,' Ellis said, playing along. 'Sorry — there might be quite a bit of overlap in what we ask. We haven't gone back and compared notes yet.'

Hardwick shot Ellis a glance, which David Campbell seemed not to notice.

'You'd think it'd all be computerised nowadays, wouldn't you?' the man said.

'Yes,' Ellis said, chuckling out loud, not quite sure what to say next. As was usually the case, he left the talking to Hardwick.

'Mr Campbell, I hope you don't mind me asking you this, but could you tell us exactly what happened between you and Veronica? In terms of the break-up and divorce, I mean.'

David Campbell sat back, took a deep breath, and exhaled heavily before speaking.

'I guess we just drifted apart, like couples do. She was always so busy with her work, and I was down in London quite a lot for mine. It just got to the point where we were more like ships in the night than a married couple.' He cleared his throat. 'Plus there might have been one or two minor things on my part. Like I say, we'd drifted apart.'

'Other women?' Hardwick asked.

'Yes. Veronica said she wasn't actually all that upset about it, and that's what told her the marriage was over. She said it felt like a friend was telling her he'd been cheating on his wife. I can still remember her using those words.'

'But she kept your surname?'

'Yeah. Sort of. Between you and me, she never knew

her real dad. Her mum married a guy when Veronica was just a toddler, and she was brought up with his surname. But he was an abusive alcoholic, so she said there was no way she was going to have his name again. She didn't have any other attachment to it. It's not like he was her real dad.'

'What about using her mother's maiden name?' Ellis asked.

David chuckled quietly. 'Campbell,' he said. 'And no, no relation, before you ask. So she might well have started using her mum's maiden name, in a funny sort of way. There's no way of telling.'

'Did you still see her regularly?' Hardwick asked.

'Not regularly, as such. We were amicable, but we didn't have children so there wasn't really anything to keep us in touch like that. But Tollinghill's a small place. I saw her around town occasionally, that sort of thing. We kept it friendly, a bit like old school friends really. Sad, in its own way.'

'And do you know if she had another partner?'

'To be honest, I didn't feel it was my place to ask. But a couple of people mentioned she was knocking around with some guy called Terry, or Tony. I don't know anything about him — didn't want to ask — but it was always said with a sort of knowing look, as though I was meant to know who he was. To be honest, I've always kept myself to myself. I do my work, come back home and relax. I've never been one for going out to the pubs or listening to the village grapevine.'

'Probably just as well,' Hardwick remarked.

'Speaking of which, Veronica was pretty much the same when we were together, but a mutual friend mentioned she'd been going out a lot since we split up. Drinking a fair bit, I think. I got a few interesting texts off her over the past few months, mostly sent late at night. Between you and me, I think she'd probably gone overboard on a few occasions.'

Hardwick cocked his head. 'What sort of texts? Do you still have them?'

'No, I don't. I deleted them. To be honest, they were pretty embarrassing. For her, I mean. There would have been no reason to keep them other than to use them against her, and I'm not that sort of person.'

'Do you remember what they said?' Ellis asked.

'Uh, some were abusive. Calling me names. Some were the complete opposite — asking if she could come and see me and show me what I was missing. Sometimes she'd flip between the two in the space of twenty minutes. Bearing in mind this was often gone midnight, it didn't take much brainpower to work out she'd been drinking.'

It seemed to Hardwick as though Veronica Campbell had been set on a course of self-destruction for some time, and that perhaps it was inevitably not going to end well. His doubts and levels of unease, though, were substantial. Something wasn't quite right. And he was going to get to the bottom of it.

'Sorry to have to ask you this, Mr Campbell,' Hardwick said, 'but where were you yesterday evening, around nine o'clock?'

Campbell smiled amiably. 'Don't worry about it. Your colleagues asked me the same question earlier. It's only natural. But I was at a business function in London. We went straight from the office at about five o'clock and I caught the twenty past ten train back from Farringdon, which got in just after eleven.'

'And that can all be backed up, presumably?'

'Well, yes. There were about thirty or forty people at the function. I travelled home on the train with two colleagues and there's CCTV all over the place. Plus I had my phone with me, so there's location data from that. Oh, and I took a cab from the station when I got back, so there's that too.'

Ellis gave Hardwick a look which told him he might just be barking up the wrong tree.

'That's very helpful,' Hardwick said. 'Thank you, Mr Campbell.'

9

Later that evening, Ellis Flint decided he'd had quite enough to drink. Following the day's detecting, he was in need of a beer or two so, naturally, took himself off to the Freemason's Arms for a few well-deserved pints.

By now, he was sure Mrs F was onto him and had noticed he'd been spending much more time at the pub but, oddly, she seemed only too pleased to see him pop out for a few hours.

He'd been mulling the day's events over in his mind, and had come to the conclusion that he was far more comfortable with the police's version of events than Hardwick had been. It seemed pretty obvious to him that Terry Cox was the main suspect, if not the only suspect.

It would be natural for the ex-husband to be a

suspect, but Ellis had immediately noticed how friendly and nice David Campbell had seemed. That counted for nothing, of course. He knew from experience that killers were often good at hiding behind facades. But he could see from Campbell's eyes and body language when he spoke about his ex-wife that there was no malice there whatsoever. Besides which, his alibi was absolutely unassailable. As was everyone's. Except for Terry Cox.

Ellis was conflicted. Although it seemed blindingly clear to him that Terry must have done it — and it was maddeningly bizarre to be chasing an alternative theory based purely on Hardwick seeing something in someone's eyes — he had to admit that his friend's hunches were often correct. In any case, it was futile trying to go against Hardwick. He was like a dog with a bone.

Stepping out of the Freemason's Arms, he began to realise that perhaps he'd drunk a little too much in too short a period of time. Going straight home wouldn't be an option. If — and it was a big if — he managed to get past Mrs F and her all-seeing eye and convince her he wasn't plastered, he'd fall asleep the second his head hit the pillow and wake up with an enormous hangover the next day. It would be better to keep himself awake for a bit longer, perhaps work off the effects of the alcohol.

He decided to take a slightly more circuitous route home, which involved heading in completely the opposite direction to his house, through Elm Walk and around the outskirts of Tollinghill, taking in as much fresh air as he could.

For the first few minutes, he felt more and more drunk, the effects accentuated by motion sickness caused by his zig-zag staggering.

He reached the end of the tree-lined walkway known as Elm Walk and fumbled with the small iron gate, which seemed for a while as if it might prove to be an unreasonably deadly nemesis. On finally unlatching it, he opened the gate as if it was his own bedroom door and Mrs F was sleeping peacefully inside, before quietly latching it and walking in the direction of the clock tower.

Tollinghill was peaceful at this time of night, and it didn't take much to alert Ellis to the movement of someone on the other side of the road. Despite his stupor, he immediately recognised Rupert Pearson. His instinct should have been to call out and greet him, but something about Pearson's body language stopped him doing so.

Ellis stepped back, allowing the shadows of the enormous trees to take him. Between him and the road was a small parking area – just enough to provide him some cover. He watched as Pearson rounded the corner and headed up a side street, trying to keep to the shadows himself.

Ellis crossed the road and followed Pearson, keeping a good distance away. He knew the author didn't live up this street — far from it — and it was an odd place to be walking at this time of the night.

He kept his eyes on Pearson at all times, and after a minute or so he watched as the man ducked down a foot-path and out of sight.

Ellis jogged to catch up, slowing as he reached the entrance to the footpath and gingerly peering round the corner. As he did so, he saw Rupert Pearson take a small key from his pocket and unlock a padlock on a wooden gate, before opening it and heading inside.

Ellis gave it a minute before walking down the foot-path and to the gate. He didn't want to try the latch. It looked as if it might be noisy. But if he stood back far enough and craned his neck upwards, he could see it was the back gate to a small house or cottage. A house or cottage to which Rupert Pearson had the keys.

10

Ellis had woken at seven o'clock that morning with a banging headache, his mobile phone ringing loudly on his face. He grabbed it, wiped the saliva from the screen with the sleeve of his pyjama top and answered it. It was Hardwick.

'Ellis, I'm going to the Freemason's Arms at nine o'clock if you want to come along.'

Ellis blinked and tried to make sense of this. 'Uh, I don't think I could get away with going out two nights in a row, Kempston,' he said.

'Not this evening, Ellis. This morning. In two hours.'

The thought of a breakfast beer made Ellis want to reach for the toilet bowl.

'This morning? Isn't that a bit early?'

'I want to catch Doug Lilley first thing. I've had a thought. There's something we need to check.'

Ellis took a deep breath, tasting last night's beer once again. He really didn't fancy going to a pub again any time soon, but he knew he didn't have much choice.

---

Ellis sucked in lungfuls of the cold morning air as he made his way through Tollinghill. He pulled his coat tightly around him, wincing slightly as he felt a dull pain in his ribs. He must've slept funny last night, he thought.

Despite the discomfort, he arrived at the Freemason's Arms at a quarter to nine, secretly hoping he'd be able to sit on the wall outside and enjoy the fresh air for fifteen minutes before Hardwick turned up. However, his private vigil was ended after no more than twenty seconds as Hardwick rounded the corner and marched towards him.

'Good morning, Ellis. Have you knocked?'

'Yeah, course. He opened the door but I just decided to stand out here in the street anyway.'

Hardwick's mouth shunted sideways slightly.

'Don't be facetious, Ellis,' he said, stepping towards the door before rapping firmly on it.

Hardwick's eyes narrowed as he looked askance at Ellis.

'Can you smell vinegar?'

Ellis blinked and shook his head. 'Not that I've noticed.'

It was a good minute or so before they saw the rotund shape of Doug Lilley walking through the pub, shaking his head as he retrieved the keys to open the door.

'Come back for more, have you?'

'Not quite. We want to double-check something with you, if we may,' Hardwick said, walking past Doug and into the Freemason's Arms.

'You may,' Doug said, to Hardwick's back, letting Ellis in behind him. 'Don't suppose you've come to apologise, have you, Ellis?'

Ellis gave Doug a quizzical look as he watched the landlord closed the door behind them. 'Apologise for what?'

'Blimey, you must have had a skinful. Derek Peterson says he saw you nicking pickled onions out of my jar and cramming them in your coat pockets.'

Hardwick sighed as Ellis plunged his hands into his pockets, finding them empty.

'Inside pockets, Ellis,' he said.

Ellis unbuttoned his coat and winced as the smell of

vinegar hit him like a freight train. Trying not to gag, he pulled six large pickled onions out of each of his inside coat pockets, immediately feeling nauseous but, on the plus side, with almost immediate relief of the dull pain in his ribs.

'We'll call in at the dry cleaner's on the way back,' Hardwick said.

'Might want to save your money and chuck it in a skip,' Doug cut in. 'Those things have been sitting on the bar untouched for a good five years now. Was a bit of a giveaway when we sold twelve in one night.'

'Sorry about that, Doug,' Ellis said, opening the jar and going to put the onions back in. 'Won't happen again.'

Doug put out a hand, leaned forward and scooped the fetid onions into a small bag, before tying it tightly and double-bagging it inside a large carrier, which he chucked into a sealed bin.

'Y'know, somehow I believe you,' he said.

'As much as I didn't think this was a sentence I'd ever say,' Hardwick said, changing the subject, 'our purpose in coming here was not to return your onions. We'd like to have a look at your CCTV.'

Doug and Ellis both looked at Hardwick with wide eyes.

'My CCTV? What for?' Doug asked.

'I just want to check a few things from the night Veronica Campbell died. Your cameras cover the inside of the pub and the road out to the front, correct?'

'Yeah. Everything except the toilets at the back, for obvious reasons.'

'How much of the road do they cover?'

'Pretty much all of it. There are two, pointing both ways down the road. You get the footpaths on both sides, too.'

'Is that legal?' Ellis asked.

'Yep, it's a public highway. The police advised us to do it in case there were any fights that spilled out into the street.'

Ellis couldn't recall a time anyone in the Freemason's Arms ever came close to fighting, although he did recall a time a couple of months back when a pensioner called his friend a git for cheating at dominos. That — apart from the brutal and horrific murder of a standup comedian a few years previous — was as animated as things got in the Freemason's.

'May we take a look?' Hardwick asked.

Doug nodded and ushered the pair behind the bar and upstairs to his office.

The office was cramped, piled high with crisp boxes and paperwork, but on a table sat a computer monitor on which eight different CCTV angles were visible.

Doug sat down and brought up a date and time selection screen. He selected the date of Veronica's death.

'What time?' he asked.

Hardwick pursed his lips. 'Veronica was in here with Terry Cox from when, would you say?'

'Pretty much opening time. But there won't be much to see until just before they left. They didn't argue until then.'

'Let's see that,' Hardwick said.

Doug rolled through the timeline as the trio watched figures darting about on the screen until the footage slowed and started to play in real time.

'Here you go,' Doug said. 'You can see the body language changing here.'

They watched as Veronica, standing at the bar, crossed her arms and turned slightly away from Terry. Terry shook his head and downed half his pint.

'Is there no sound?' Ellis asked.

'Nope. You wouldn't want to hear half the stuff people talk about in here anyway.'

Doug sped the footage up to four times the actual speed, and it became clear the exchange between Veronica and Terry was getting more and more heated. After a short while, he slowed it back down to real time.

'Here you go. You can see him jabbing his finger in the air. Look at her face. She ain't happy.'

Hardwick murmured his agreement.

'I don't think this was long before she walked out. Yep, here you go, she's picking up her coat.'

On the screen, Veronica stood and headed for the front door of the pub. Terry took a moment to sink the rest of his pint before following her.

Doug changed the view to the outside cameras. As the pair were standing right outside the front door, they were visible from both camera angles, which were set up to cross in front of each other, ensuring no areas were left uncovered.

'This is where they start having a barney out in the street. You can see kids in school uniform over on the other side of the street, look. And here we go. The wanderer returns.'

Doug smirked as he pointed to the top corner of one of the boxes, the unmistakeable figure of Hardwick walking into shot.

'They weren't arguing for long before you turned up, then,' Ellis said.

'Don't worry about me, Ellis. We need to see what happened next with them.'

On the screen, Veronica turned as if right on cue and headed off down the street in the direction of South

Heath. Terry glanced after her, seemed to consider himself for a moment, then followed her.

They watched as the pair headed towards the edge of the screen before disappearing.

'Is that it?' Hardwick asked.

'Yep. I can't cover the whole of Tollinghill.'

Hardwick sat for a moment and thought.

'We don't know where Veronica and Terry were going, but they were heading in the direction of South Heath and Veronica's body was found up at the park, correct?'

'Yes.'

'Correct me if I'm wrong, but there are a number of different ways they could have got to the park. They could have gone up Elm Walk, Ridgeway Road or down into the centre of town and up Park Road. Presuming they didn't take a three mile detour and walk along the length of the Tollinghill bypass, each of those routes would have meant they'd have to have walked past the pub again on the way.'

Doug and Ellis thought for a moment, and nodded. Hardwick was right. Tollinghill sat atop a hill ridge, and much of the small town consisted of dips and rises which meant Tollinghill had organically developed around these geological oddities. As a result, all streets heading west off the South Heath Road were cul-de-sacs, with the land then dipping heavily before rising again just before the western bypass. This made that side of town unsuitable for any footpaths or bridleways.

'Fast-forward the footage, Doug. Let's have a look and see when they headed back this way.'

Doug did as Hardwick asked, and the three watched as the figures skitted about on the screen, just fleetingly enough to be able to spot anyone recognisable, but not slowly enough to ensure they were going to be sitting there all day.

'There!' Hardwick barked, making Doug throw his computer mouse halfway across the room.

Once it had been retrieved, Doug wound the footage back to the point Hardwick had identified. It was unmistakeable — Veronica Campbell was walking back past the pub, talking into her mobile phone. She slowed slightly as she passed the pub, glancing in the window and then looking at her watch before continuing on her way.

'Must have been checking to see how long she had before the launch party,' Ellis said.

'Well observed, Ellis. It rather seems to indicate that Veronica at least intended to be there.'

They watched as the footage continued, people walking past the front of the Freemason's Arms at double speed, until Doug paused the video again.

'That's him,' he said, quietly, the unspoken words clear to them all. Terry Cox was walking back past the pub, in the same direction Veronica had passed barely a minute or so earlier.

'In the direction of the park,' Ellis said.

Hardwick murmured. 'Loosely. There are a number of places they could have been going. They could even have been going to completely different locations.'

'Bit of a coincidence, though, isn't it?'

Hardwick lifted his head and looked at Ellis and Doug.

'Let's find out.'

11

Hardwick led Ellis and Doug back downstairs and out to the front of the pub.

'Doug, do you have a stopwatch?' he asked.

'Uh, I've got one on my phone I think.'

'Ellis?'

'Yeah, same,' Ellis replied.

'Good. Ellis, I want you to walk down the road in the direction of the town centre. Don't take any of the side roads — just keep walking. Give it at least a minute, then you can turn around and come back.'

Ellis gave Hardwick a quizzical look, but did as he was told.

Hardwick gave Doug a nod of his head and the landlord started his stopwatch running. After thirty seconds or so, Hardwick made a throaty noise and pursed his lips.

'Interesting.'

'What is?' Doug asked.

'Would you say he's walking about the same speed as Veronica Campbell was walking on the CCTV footage we just watched?'

Doug looked down the road. 'Yeah, I suppose so. A bit slower, if anything.'

'Indeed. But look what the hill and the bend in the road does. He's almost disappeared from sight already. Get ready to stop the clock, Doug. Three. Two. One. Stop.'

Hardwick adjusted his coat and turned to Doug, who showed him the time on his phone screen. Hardwick raised his eyebrows, gave Doug a small smile and waited for Ellis to return.

When he finally did, any passer-by would assume the man had just run a marathon as opposed to walking a hundred yards or so.

'Very interesting indeed, Ellis,' Hardwick boomed as his friend approached. 'Forty-eight seconds.'

'What was?' Ellis puffed.

'The time it took for you to completely disappear from sight. Now, you're not the tallest chap in the world but I believe I'm right in saying Veronica Campbell was slightly shorter, so she would have gained an extra half-second or so in the invisibility stakes. On the CCTV footage, Terry Cox was seventy-two seconds behind Veronica when he walked past the pub. There's no way he could have seen Veronica from that distance. And that's if she carried on walking in a straight line towards the town centre. If she came off the main road and walked up Elm Walk or Ridgeway Road, it would be even more unlikely.'

Ellis shuffled awkwardly. 'They had a massive barney right here in the pub, Kempston. You saw them out in the street when you came in. They walked off together, then Veronica comes back past the pub, towards the park where she's later found murdered, followed by Terry. I've got to be honest, I really can't see why you've got such a bee in your bonnet about this.'

'But that's just the point, Ellis. Veronica *wasn't* followed by Terry. He couldn't see her. She was too far ahead of him, and the curvature of the road doesn't allow for it. It's a coincidence that he walked down the same street a minute after her.'

'Doesn't mean he didn't kill her though,' Doug said.

'True. Nothing proves or disproves anyone's guilt yet. But it does go to show that every piece of so-called evidence gathered so far is purely coincidental.'

'As far as we know,' Ellis added. 'I mean, we don't

know what evidence the police have got. Presumably something.'

'The overwhelming likelihood is that they've got absolutely nothing, Ellis. They don't need any evidence to arrest somebody, but they need compelling evidence to charge them. In the case of murder, they could detain Terry Cox for a maximum of ninety-six hours — after jumping through all sorts of hoops to get continual extension on the standard twenty-four. As I understand it, they've still not charged him or released him, so they're still applying for extensions and still gathering evidence. Which means they don't yet have enough evidence to charge him. Which *certainly* means they don't yet have enough evidence to convict him.'

'But they arrested him,' Doug said. 'That means he must have done it.'

Hardwick stopped breathing for a moment and looked at Doug. 'Sorry, perhaps I just said all that in my head. Because I thought I made it pretty clear that patently isn't the case.'

'No smoke without fire,' Ellis added, helpfully.

'And it's remarks like that which ruin people's lives, Ellis. Anybody can be arrested for anything at any time. All it does is give the police time to speak with you on the record. It's a legal requirement under the Police and Criminal Evidence Act. Without interviewing you under caution, nothing you say can be used as evidence. They don't even need to suspect you of committing a crime. Any one of us could be arrested right now, for any crime at all. I don't think you'd be saying there was no smoke without fire then, Ellis. There but for the grace of God go I.'

'So what are you saying? That Terry's innocent?' Doug asked.

'No, I'm saying that nobody can possibly say either way at the moment. The only person who knows who killed Veronica Campbell is her killer. And so far all we've managed to do is build up a picture of who that person isn't. All we've got are coincidences and like-lihoods.'

'So what next?' Ellis said, after a brief period of silence.

Hardwick gazed off onto the horizon and narrowed his eyes. 'That's a very good question, Ellis.'

12

'Ellis, lend me your mobile phone,' Hardwick said as they walked away from the Freemason's Arms towards the centre of Tollinghill.

Ellis sighed and dipped his hand into his trouser pocket.

'You need to get one of your own. Seriously.'

'I don't need one, Ellis. I manage perfectly well without.'

'Yeah, you do when you can borrow someone else's every five minutes.'

'You get free calls, don't you?' Hardwick asked.

'Yes, but that's not the point.'

'Then what is the point?'

Ellis struggled to formulate an answer before Hardwick had finished dialling the number and had his call answered.

'Ah, hello. I'd like to speak to Detective Inspector Warner, please,' Hardwick said into the phone. 'Yes, my name's Kempston Hardwick. Thank you.'

A few seconds later, his call was patched through.

'Detective Inspector Warner,' Hardwick said, sounding overenthusiastically friendly.

'What is it, Kempston?' Warner said, not sounding quite as enthusiastic himself.

'I just wondered if you had any news on the Veronica Campbell case. We've been speaking to a few people and doing some investigating of our own and we've discovered a few little oddities.'

Hardwick heard Warner sighing heavily on the other end of the line.

'The only oddity around here is you,' he said. 'What do you mean you've been speaking to people?'

'Sorry, Inspector. I didn't realise it was illegal to speak to people.'

'It's not, but it is illegal to pretend to be a police officer.'

'I've never pretended to be a police officer,' Hardwick said. 'Far from it.'

'*DI* Kempston Hardwick?'

'Yes, it's my name. What of it?'

'You're sailing very close to the wind, Hardwick.'

'It's where all the best waves are, Inspector.'

There was a moment of silence before Warner spoke.

'You know I can't give you any news. Anything that's released for public knowledge goes out through the press. If it hasn't been released, it's not something I can tell you.'

'Well that rather makes our little arrangement null and void then, doesn't it?'

He could practically hear Warner squirming on the other end of the line.

'You do know blackmail is illegal, don't you? And blackmailing a serving police officer is a hundred times worse.'

'I don't believe I've blackmailed anyone, Inspector. For that, I'd need to have told you I'd do something unpleasant if you didn't share your information with me. As it happens, I've done nothing of the sort.'

'You know exactly what you've done,' Warner said, his voice almost a whisper.

'We're both completely free to share information with other people, Inspector. How is Mrs Warner, by the way?'

Hardwick's question was met with a deathly silence. It was a good ten seconds before Warner spoke again.

'You do realise I could end you right now, don't you, Hardwick?'

'Yes, I do. And I'm quite sure the feeling's mutual. So. Veronica Campbell. Terry Cox. What can you tell me?'

Warner sighed. 'He was arrested for her murder.'

'Truly enlightening, Inspector. Has he been charged?'

'Not yet, no.'

'But not released?'

'No.'

'So presumably there's enough that your superiors, and probably a magistrate at this stage,' Hardwick said, glancing at his watch, 'are happy to keep him in custody. But not quite enough to authorise a charge. No DNA or forensic evidence, then?'

'Don't sound so smug, Hardwick. The only reason for that is that the forensics reports haven't come back yet. There's been a backlog, and we've already had one set come back inconclusive.'

Hardwick cocked his head. 'Inconclusive? What does that mean?'

'It means they couldn't come to a conclusion either way.'

'I know what the word means, Inspector. I mean

what would cause the results to come back as incon-clusive?'

'Could be anything. We don't know yet.'

'Does Cox have an alibi?'

'Yes and no. He claims he was at home all evening, sleeping off the drink. On his own, of course.'

'Mobile phone records?'

'His phone was home all day anyway. He dropped it down the toilet that morning. It was drying out.'

'Him and his phone both, eh? Handy, though.'

'We seized the phone. It's wrecked. The water damage and GPS history backs up his story in that regard.'

'So what actually places him at the scene, Inspector? Because the more we look at this, the more we find things which contradict that assumption.'

Warner was silent for a moment.

'I can't go into detail on that, Hardwick.'

'But presumably there were blood spatters on his clothes? It's hard to beat someone to death without getting blood everywhere. That would be the sort of thing I expect would be strong enough evidence to extend a suspect's detention, but falling short of a DNA match in order to charge.'

'It would be, yes,' Warner said, non-commitally.

'But you're not going to tell me that's what happened, are you?'

Warner sighed again.

'Look, there are things I'd love to be able to tell you. Believe me. But I can't. I'll give you what I'd be able to give civilian support staff, but I can't do anything else. You'd be asking me to put my entire career on the line.'

Hardwick pondered this for a moment, but decided it would be better to accept what Warner had to say for now. There was plenty of time. Hardwick always lived by the maxim that no wise person should profit today at the expense of tomorrow.

'You'll give me a call back when you hear something, won't you Inspector? Or when you have something else you feel you might be able to share with me. I think it would be in both our interests.'

Hardwick could picture Warner shoving his tongue into the inside of his cheek to stop himself losing his cool.

'Yeah,' the inspector said, eventually. 'Yeah, I'll give you a call if there's anything that might help.'

13

'Anything useful?' Ellis asked, as Hardwick handed him back his phone.

'Absolutely nothing whatsoever, unsurprisingly,' Hardwick said. 'But at least Detective Inspector Warner knows where everyone stands.'

'So what now?'

'Now we need to sit down and assimilate everything we know. The most important things are to ascertain where everyone was at ten past nine on the night Veronica died. We need to know their movements before and after then, too. Sticking rigidly to known patterns can be just as suspicious as behaving slightly out of the ordinary.'

Ellis nodded slowly. 'Like Pearson visiting that cottage, for example.'

'What cottage?' Hardwick asked, slowing his pace slightly.

'The one I saw Pearson going into last night. I told you.'

Hardwick stopped. 'No, Ellis, you certainly didn't. But I think you'd better tell me everything.'

'I came out of the pub last night and I saw Pearson.'

'Where?'

'At the end of Elm Walk.'

'But that's nowhere near your route home.'

'I know. I was getting a bit of fresh air. Trying to sober up a bit. Anyway, I saw Pearson on the other side of the road. Something about it just made me suspicious, so I followed him. He went up a little side alley and in through the back gate of a cottage.'

'Do you know which one?'

'No, but I could find it again,' Ellis said.

'In that case,' Hardwick said, starting up his pace again and heading in the direction of Elm Walk, 'we'd better get going.'

14

As they made their way towards the cottage Ellis had seen Rupert Pearson enter the previous night, Ellis began to feel nervous.

He always felt nervous when Hardwick had just realised or uncovered a new piece of information. Hardwick was like a dog with a bone at times, and Ellis never quite knew what he was going to do with his latest discovery.

The problem with Hardwick, Ellis thought, was that his friend had a rather unconventional take on social boundaries. Sure, Ellis was no David Niven — he'd readily admit as much himself — but there was no denying that Kempston Hardwick was... odd.

Ellis Flint had met many odd people in pubs. There

were many odd people in Tollinghill, and many pubs. The probability of the two colliding were unnaturally high. But this was the sort of thing which tended to give villages and small towns their quirks.

And Tollinghill certainly had its quirks.

It made a good effort of putting on an impressive face and showing allcomers its impressive Georgian buildings and chic market square. It did a wonderful job, too, of hiding its inevitable and inescapable sordid side far down the backstreets and behind closed doors.

No town was free of unsavouriness. Where there were people, there was dishonour and disrepute.

Ellis had never really considered this until he'd met Kempston Hardwick. In many ways, the last eight years had been the most fascinating and insightful of his life. In others, he wanted to slap Kempston for sullying his view of the world.

That was the sort of innocence he'd never completely regain, although he did a wonderful job of trying to see the positives in all walks of life. Compared to Kempston Hardwick, though, a street-corner doom-monger declaring the end of times would seem like an optimist.

There was something inescapably compelling about the man, though. An air of mystery that had been apparent from the first moment he'd met him in the Freemason's Arms eight years earlier.

In all the time he'd known Kempston, he realised he'd never actually got to know him. He knew barely anything more about the man now than he did eight years previous. To say Kempston Hardwick kept himself to himself was an understatement.

Ellis felt far more exposed approaching the cottage in broad daylight than he had sneaking around the back-streets of Tollinghill under cover of darkness last night. He didn't tend to have the same instinctive reactions as Hardwick, but there was no doubting that something felt wrong about Rupert Pearson's behaviour. It wasn't something he could put his finger on, but it was definitely there.

'This one, I think,' Ellis said, gesturing with his head towards one of the garden gates.

'Presumably there's a front door,' Hardwick replied, turning and heading back in the direction from which they'd just come, before rounding the corner and walking up the road in front of the cottages. 'Third one up, yes?' he said, stopping outside the cottage they both assumed was the one Pearson had entered. It had a low, white picket fence surrounding it and a few unkempt shrubs in the otherwise lawned front garden.

'I think so,' Ellis replied.

'Well, no time like the present,' Hardwick said, unlatching the low front gate and marching up the front path.

'Kempston, no! You can't just go—'

It was no use even protesting. Before Ellis had finished his sentence, Hardwick was already rapping loudly at the door, before stepping backwards and looking at the upstairs windows.

Each of the windows — upstairs and down — was draped with a net curtain, making it difficult to see inside. The general look and feel of the property gave Hardwick the impression that the person who lived here was not young or particularly active. That, in his mind, rather reduced the likelihood that this was where Rupert Pearson's secret lover lived — although it took all sorts.

Hardwick stepped onto the front lawn, leaned across the flowerbed which sat under one of the front windows, and attempted to peer inside.

The angle of the light was terrible, and the thick net curtains certainly weren't helping any.

'See anything?' Ellis asked.

'No. Although to be honest there could be a party in full swing inside there and I doubt I'd be able to see anything.'

'You'd be able to hear it, though,' Ellis replied, without a hint of humour in his voice.

'Yes. Yes, Ellis, I would.'

'Maybe they're not in.'

'On the contrary,' Hardwick replied, kneeling down by the door. 'There's a key on the inside of this lock.'

Ellis crouched down next to him to take a look. He was right. The lock was an old-style traditional lock — not one of the new Yale-style latches. It, rather handily, left a sizeable keyhole-shaped keyhole in the doorframe, through which Hardwick and Flint could see the lock was already occupied.

'So why aren't they answering?'

'You tell me, Ellis. Guilt. Infirmity. Social ineptitude.'

'Is that why you don't answer your door nine times out of ten?'

'No, that's because I know that eight times out of ten it'll be you.'

'And what about the other one?'

'One has to leave some things to chance, Ellis.'

Ellis stood on the front path, not entirely sure what to say next, looking at Hardwick for some sort of guidance or inspiration. He daren't ask, though. He'd learned to be careful about things like that. For all he knew,

Hardwick would take it as a suggestion that they break into the cottage.

Hardwick sighed. 'I think we're going to have to come back another time, Ellis. In the meantime, I do have one idea.'

15

'But I'll freeze to death!' Ellis said.

'Nonsense. It's quite mild in the evenings now. Anyway, you probably won't have to stand out there for long.'

'And how are we meant to know when he's going to go back there next?'

'We're not. That's why it might take a few days to find the perfect opportunity.'

'And what if there never is a perfect opportunity?'

'There always is. Don't you worry about that.'

The pair were now almost at the Old Rectory, Ellis struggling to keep up with the marching Hardwick.

Hardwick's grand plan had been for Ellis to revisit the area each evening around the same time and lie in wait for Pearson. When he saw him, he'd call Hardwick, who would come and join him. Then they'd decide what to do — apprehend Pearson or wait until he'd left before trying to enter the cottage through the back gate.

Hardwick pushed open his own creaking black iron gate and walked up the steep stepped path towards the front door of the Old Rectory, where he lived. He took a key out of his pocket and unlocked the door, before pushing it open and stepping inside, the doorway leaking the loud sound of a phone ringing inside.

Ellis went to step in after him, just as Hardwick began to close the door.

'Oh, charming.'

'Are you still here, Ellis? I thought you were going into town.'

'Why? I didn't say anything about going into town.'

'Oh, right. My mistake. Anyway, I must get on.'

'Can't I come in, then?'

Hardwick stood and looked at Ellis, his blinking getting faster.

'Phone's ringing, Kempston. Might want to get that.'

Hardwick grunted and headed inside the house, leaving the door open for Ellis.

He headed through and into the living room, where Hardwick was already sitting in a large wingback chair, the vintage telephone to his ear as he mumbled something to the person on the other end of the line.

Ellis took a moment to look around him. He couldn't recall how many times he'd set foot inside the Old Rectory, but he doubted if this was even the third. Hardwick's quest for privacy meant he didn't tend to invite anyone to his place, but Ellis had managed to insist on entry once or twice in the past eight years.

The walls of the living room and dining room were almost completely hidden by bookcases, each stacked high with books, the shelves creaking under the weight of the hefty tomes. No wonder he didn't have time to read much Rupert Pearson, Ellis thought. He had this lot to get through first.

Walking into Kempston Hardwick's house was like walking back in time. The building itself, the Old Rectory, was, of course, old. It made perfect sense for its occupant to furnish it with antique furniture and curios, but there seemed to Ellis to be no sense of fashion or thought behind its style. It's not that it was gaudy or untidy — just that it was clear Hardwick hadn't styled the Old Rectory in this way as a fashion statement, but because this was genuinely how the man liked to live.

Ellis couldn't spot a single item here that he had in his own house — or that he'd ever seen before. Hardwick could quite conceivably hire out his house to film crews looking for ready-made sets for period dramas.

In any case, it was clear to Ellis that Hardwick was a

man who liked to do things properly. In the corner of the large lounge was a writing bureau, stacked with blank high-quality writing paper. In the centre of the bureau was an ornate wooden display box containing what Ellis guessed was around twenty or thirty fountain pens. Behind it was a row of a dozen bottles of ink. Although he didn't take much time to look, he knew there wouldn't be a single rollerball in this entire building, much less something so distasteful to Hardwick as a plastic Bic.

'Thank you,' Hardwick murmured a little while later, before placing the receiver back on the unit and sitting in silence.

'Who was that?' Ellis asked, noting that Hardwick didn't look particularly happy.

'Detective Inspector Warner,' Hardwick replied.

'What did he want?'

'To gloat, Ellis. He told me they found Terry Cox's DNA all over Veronica's body and hers all over his. No blood, but plenty of hairs and other fibres which showed they'd been in very close proximity.'

Ellis's eyes narrowed. 'Well, obviously. They were lovers.'

'Exactly.'

'Didn't you tell him that?'

'And what would be the point, hmm? He's telling us for one of two reasons: either he's desperately trying to convince us he's got the right man and throw us off the scent or he's actually stupid enough to believe that "evidence" wouldn't get torn to shreds by a defence barrister with at least thirty seconds' experience. I'll leave you to draw your own conclusions as to which is true.'

'What, so you're saying we sit back and let it get to court and watch Terry walk free? If that's the case, there's still a killer out there somewhere, Kempston. We can't just do nothing.'

'I'm not suggesting for one minute we do nothing, Ellis. I'm suggesting we give Detective Inspector Warner the impression we're going to do nothing. There would be no strategic advantage to anything other than nodding and smiling. We need to take him something far stronger than "We think you're wrong".'

Before Ellis could process this, he felt his mobile phone vibrating in his inside jacket pocket. He recognised the number on the screen immediately.

'Hello?' he said, sheepishly, while he listened to the voice on the other end of the phone. 'That was Doug,' he said, when the call was finished. 'From the pub. He said to tell you he had another look at the footage from the night Veronica died — from later in the evening. Terry Cox walked back past the pub after the time Veronica died.'

'And?'

'And he was wearing the same clothes. If that's the case, they would have been covered in blood!'

'Could he see from the footage?' Hardwick asked.

'No, the quality's not that good and it was dark, but it was definitely him and definitely the same clothes.'

'So why wasn't Veronica's blood found on Terry Cox or any item of clothing he was wearing that night?'

'Because he didn't do it, obviously,' Ellis replied.

'Indeed,' Hardwick replied, staring off into the middle distance and stroking his chin. 'Indeed.'

16

Kempston Hardwick made his way from Tollinghill Country Park towards the police station, by now certain that Terry Cox could not have killed Veronica Campbell.

The evidence against him was all circumstantial, whereas that in his favour was overwhelming. And now that Hardwick had visited the scene of the crime in relative peace and quiet, without the continual noise and distraction of Ellis Flint, he'd been even further convinced of Terry Cox's innocence.

There were things which DI Warner was shrugging off as irrelevant because they didn't prove Cox's guilt, whereas Hardwick concluded that they went one huge step further and proved his innocence.

For example, there was no way Cox could have

killed Veronica without splattering himself with blood. They now knew he didn't change his clothes, so the clothes he was known to have worn that night would have contained blood spatters. None, so far, had been found.

By now, the case in Cox's favour had gone beyond Hardwick's initial instinct that Terry Cox was not a killer, although he did take some not insignificant pride in being able to say that he'd been right.

But there was something else he'd noticed at Tollinghill Country Park which hadn't crossed his mind until then. And that was something he now intended to bring up with DI Warner.

The receptionist's face dropped as Hardwick walked into the police station. 'I'll go and get him,' she said, before disappearing through a door and down a corridor.

A minute or so later, the door opened and DI Warner beckoned him through.

'You'll have to keep this quick, Hardwick. I've got a lot on today.'

'Yes, I should imagine you do. By my reckoning you've got, what, just under four hours left to charge or release Terry Cox. Even after the extensions you've had, you must be starting to get a little nervous.'

'I don't get nervous,' Warner replied. 'I don't have time for it. Anyway, if you think this is the trickiest job

I've ever worked on you can think again. It's perfectly normal practice for us to want to get all our ducks in a row before going to the CPS.'

'Must be an awful lot of ducks,' Hardwick said, 'How did you get the magistrate to swing the final extension? That takes quite some doing.'

Warner pushed open the door to his office. 'Magistrates are very busy people. We find they're becoming more and more receptive to taking the police's word for it when it comes to issuing warrants and stuff. Shame you're not capable of doing the same.'

Hardwick smiled. 'On the contrary, Detective Inspector. I'm perfectly capable of believing the truth. But I'm also more than able to gather and collate evidence, piece together a meticulous picture of what happened or didn't happen and come to a conclusion which accurately reflects the truth. It's a shame you're not capable of doing the same.'

Warner sighed and sat down in his chair without offering Hardwick a seat. 'Let's not waste my time playing word tennis, Hardwick. I can use a thesaurus as well as anybody. What do you want?'

'I want to help you.'

Warner looked at him and snorted. 'You want to help me? What possible help do you think you could give me exactly?'

'I want to help you not embarrass yourself by pursuing this ridiculous assumption that Terry Cox must have killed Veronica Campbell.'

'What, all because you saw innocence in his sweet blue eyes? Sorry Hardwick, we don't act on hunches or feelings. We prefer this little thing called evidence.'

Hardwick smiled and sat down opposite him. 'Good. Because I've managed to gather plenty of that, too.'

Warner cocked his head. 'Go on then.'

'Firstly, CCTV footage from the Freemason's Arms. I presume you've viewed it?'

'Yes, thanks. It showed Terry and Veronica having a flaming great row outside the pub earlier that day. Witnesses in the pub said they'd been drinking heavily.'

'Correct. Did you look at the footage of everything that happened after?' Hardwick could see in Warner's eyes that he hadn't.

'Which bit?' Warner asked.

'The bit where Terry Cox and Veronica Campbell walk back past the pub towards the centre of Tollinghill.'

'Where he followed her, you mean. Yes, I've been told about that.'

'He wasn't following her. There's no way he could have even seen her — he was too far behind. It's a sheer coincidence they were walking along the same road.'

Warner chuckled to himself. 'You do like your coincidences, don't you? It's a coincidence he followed her to the park. It's a coincidence they had a bloody great row a couple of hours earlier, it's a coincidence he was drinking heavily and is known to be violent. But Kempston effing Hardwick turns up and declares he looked into the man's eyes and saw Mahatma Gandhi and everything else can go to muck. That's about the long and short of it, isn't it?'

'I wouldn't have said so, Detective Inspector, but I appreciate the sentiment. What I was going to say is that Terry Cox can be seen on the CCTV footage walking back past the pub, towards his house, not long after Veronica Campbell was murdered.'

'Walking back from killing her, you mean,' Warner said.

'That's where it becomes interesting. What we *can* see is that Terry Cox was wearing the exact same clothes we saw him in earlier in the footage: an off-white denim jacket and blue jeans. No accounting for taste, but there we are. My point is that if he was wearing those clothes throughout the attack, they'd be spattered with blood.'

'Maybe he changed to kill her.'

'Into what? Some clothes he'd secreted somewhere in the park?'

'He could have gone home to get changed.'

'Not without passing the CCTV camera outside the Freemason's Arms.'

'Maybe he went to a friend's.'

'Yes, perhaps. "Sorry, old chap. Can I just pop in and change into some of your clothes? Got a quick murder to do."'

'There's no need to be facetious, Hardwick.'

Hardwick sat back in his chair. 'So you *were* right, Detective Inspector.'

Warner's eyes narrowed. 'About what?'

'You *are* good with a thesaurus.'

Warner crossed his arms. 'Y'know, my mother used to say that the first person to resort to insults has lost the argument.'

'That's fascinating, Detective Inspector. As I was saying, Terry Cox's clothes would undoubtedly be covered in blood. I mean, if he killed Veronica there must at the very least be a small spatter somewhere on one of the items of clothing, no?'

'Like I said on the phone, nothing found so far. But —' Warner added, raising his palm to stop Hardwick from interjecting, 'that doesn't mean they won't find it. Terry Cox has been in trouble with the police before. He knows how these things work. He'll have done his best to cover his tracks and hide things from us. Protective clothing, perhaps. But we'll find it. Don't you worry about that.'

'Yes, maybe you'll find the little pink pinafore he put on before bludgeoning his girlfriend to death. Funny you should mention tracks, though, Detective Inspector. That brings me on to my next point. I went up to Tollinghill Country Park before I came to see you. It's not somewhere I go often, which is a shame considering it's practically on my doorstep.'

'How nice for you. You should have told me, I'd have brought a picnic.'

'And what I noticed is that the ground is remarkably wet and sticky around the area where Veronica Camp-bell's body was found.'

'Yes, it's called mud. It does that.'

'Not when it hasn't rained, it doesn't. In fact, the last rainfall we had in Tollinghill was the day before Veronica Campbell was murdered. It rained incessantly the whole day, great rivulets of water running down the street.'

Warner nodded his head. 'I remember.'

'It rained so much, in fact, the ground near the murder site is still wet and sticky even now. It's quite a shaded area, though. Boggy, almost. The grass doesn't grow particularly well. That means footprints are very easily left in the mud.'

'Funny you should say that,' Warner said, his interest piqued. 'We found footprints at the scene. We're still working to get the model of shoe identified. Some cheap Chinese import from Amazon or eBay, we think, but they were size nines — the same size Terry Cox wears.'

'Along with half of Tollinghill, I daresay. Myself included.'

'I can add you to the list of suspects if you like.'

'List?'

'You know what I mean, Hardwick. But yes, there were footprints. And yes, we think they were Terry's.'

'You've found the shoes, then?'

'Not yet, no. I imagine he threw them away. Like I say, he knows how these things work.'

'He was wearing white trainers on the CCTV footage. The landlord at the Freemason's Arms reckoned they looked new. You can see them fairly clearly in the latest footage when Terry Cox walks back past the Freemason's Arms from the direction of the park, towards his house — after Veronica Campbell's murder.'

'So what?' Warner asked.

'They still looked new to me, Detective Inspector. No sign of them being caked in mud. Unlike these, you might note.'

Hardwick pushed his chair back, lifted his right leg

and brought it crashing down on Warner's desk. Bits of mud flew off, one landing in the inspector's mug of coffee.

'Here, what the bloody hell are you playing at?'

'Detective Inspector, I walked from Tollinghill Country Park, down the hill and into the police station. Terry Cox wouldn't have walked much further before he was seen on CCTV passing the Freemason's Arms shortly after Veronica Campbell was murdered. The ground would have been much wetter, much muddier and much sticker that night than it was earlier today. But, as you can see, my shoes are absolutely caked with mud. On that CCTV footage, Terry Cox's white training shoes are exactly that — pure white. There is no way on this earth that Terry Cox went anywhere near so much as a shallow puddle, never mind the quagmire that part of Tollinghill Country Park would've been that night.'

Warner leaned forward on the desk, closing the gap between the two men. 'Listen here. I'm not going to say this again. We have witnesses showing Terry and Veronica arguing in public. We've got CCTV evidence backing it up. The same CCTV evidence that shows Terry following Veronica in the direction of the park.'

'Hours before she was killed,' Hardwick interjected.

'We've got their DNA all over each other.'

'As you'd expect from a couple in an intimate rela-
tionship.'

'Back off, Hardwick!'

The pair sat in silence for a few moments before
Hardwick spoke.

'You know the CPS won't authorise a charge in a
million years, don't you? Especially not if they're made
aware of the conditions at the site, to the point where the
lack of mud on Terry Cox's shoes and clothing could go
so far as to prove his innocence.'

'Absence of evidence is not evidence of absence.
That's drilled into police officers from day one. I'm sorry
that members of the *public* aren't given the same training,' Warner replied, with a sneer.

'Under normal circumstances, I'd agree. But the
conditions at Tollinghill Country Park that night were
not normal circumstances. I'm certain the Crown Prosecution Service would agree. If they knew all the facts.'

Warner's eyes narrowed. 'Are you threatening me?'

'Absolutely not, Detective Inspector. We're just
chewing the fat, are we not? I'm guessing from the fact
that you've applied for numerous extensions to Terry
Cox's custody time that you're hopeful of a charge. Of
course, for that to happen you'd have to withhold the
information about the conditions at the park and the lack
of evidence linking Terry Cox to the scene of the crime.

That wouldn't be an ideal set of circumstances either, would it? That would almost certainly put your job on the line if it were ever to get out.'

Warner pursed his lips. 'Cox did it. I'm certain of it.'

'Human beings aren't infallible, Detective Inspector. We're often wrong.'

'And you count yourself in that, do you?'

'Some are wrong more often than others. Admittedly, I'm rarely wrong.'

'I had a feeling you might say that. Listen, I've come across Terry Cox far too many times in the past. You might have looked into his eyes once and seen a veritible Mother Teresa, but I know what he's really like. There'll be evidence, don't you worry.'

'Enough to convict him?'

'More than enough.'

Hardwick lifted his arm, looked at his watch and made an approving noise. 'In which case, you're going to have to find it pretty quickly, aren't you, Detective Inspector? Tick tock.'

17

Ellis Flint was convinced his wife got up during the night to deliberately hide important items around the house. Nothing was ever where he left it, even though she swore blind she hadn't touched it. She'd accuse him of having a 'man look', which usually resulted in him going back to the first place he'd looked for the item and finding it sitting right there, almost smirking at him.

He was a man who was perfectly used to feeling foolish from time to time, but Mrs F did a wonderful job of making him look daft on a regular basis. Fortunately for him, he wasn't the sort of person to take it to heart or feel emasculated. He'd got used to the idea of his wife being the breadwinner — as she had been for many years — and counted himself as a thoroughly modern man.

His nephews weren't so sure, though. According to

them, a middle-aged man wearing shoes with no socks wasn't the done thing. He'd even (briefly) taken to wearing a waist bag diagonally across his chest after accidentally logging onto Instagram and seeing a young person doing it. His nephews had quickly told him he definitely shouldn't do that, and were even less convinced when he told them he thought he looked 'on fleek'.

He didn't know what it was with kids these days. If you talked about adult stuff they looked as though their eyes had just glazed over; if you tried to get on a level with them they scoffed as if he'd just claimed two plus two was seven.

Generally speaking, Ellis couldn't make much sense of the world. Which is why he didn't bother. He'd long ago given up worrying about inconsequential things, and he felt much happier as a result.

He wasn't feeling particularly happy now, though, as he hunted through the cutlery drawer for his missing phone charger. It was a good job Mrs F wasn't here, else his troubles would be compounded with helpful comments like 'Have you tried the plug socket?'

He'd just about managed to dislodge the fork which had jammed its way into the lip of the drawer unit and prevented the drawer from opening fully when the doorbell rang.

He walked from his kitchen into the hallway — spotting the phone charger nestled in the plug socket — and went to answer the door. He recognised the figure on the other side of the frosted glass immediately.

'Ah, Ellis. Just the man,' Hardwick said, pushing past him and into the hallway. 'Get your shoes on.'

'Why? Where are we going?'

'To Veronica Campbell's house. I did try calling you, but it went to voicemail.'

'Well yes, my phone's died. I was trying to—'

'Come on, chop chop. Time is of the essence.'

'Not really,' Ellis said, forcing on a pair of outsized loafers. 'She's been dead for days.'

'Exactly. Which is why now's the time to strike.'

---

It didn't take long to walk from Ellis Flint's house to Veronica Campbell's cottage. Then again, nothing was a particularly long walk in Tollinghill.

It was a beautiful-looking building. Ellis imagined David Campbell must have been pretty cut up about having to move out of here and into his new place on Laurel Street. Veronica's ex-husband gave them the impression that he'd certainly moved on, but there was no way he can't have been pained to have left a property like this.

It sat in a row of very similar cottages, all with thatched roofs, timber frames and wonky windows. Ellis wouldn't like to hazard a guess at how old these cottages were, but they certainly hadn't been thrown up in the past few years. This was the oldest part of Tollinghill, the area from which the not inconsiderable housing sprawl had started.

'How are you planning on getting in, Kempston? Veronica lived on her own. She's not exactly going to answer the door, is she?'

'I've got a key, Ellis.'

'A key?' Ellis asked, confused.

'Of sorts, yes.'

Hardwick marched up to the front door, took something out of his pocket and spent a few seconds fiddling with the lock before the door popped open.

'Did you just pick that lock?' Ellis asked.

'No comment, Ellis. Although I did check the lock yesterday to make sure it was as insecure as I'd hoped.'

'How on earth did you do that without being spotted?'

'I got some leaflets printed and put one through each door on the street. It was the only way I could get close enough to inspect the lock. Oh, and if anyone invites you to a meeting on how the teachings of Shintoism could impact climate change, don't go. It doesn't exist.'

'What, climate change?'

'No, Ellis. The meeting.'

The pair entered the cottage and closed the door behind them. Ellis was astounded that they hadn't been approached by a neighbour yet. You only needed to stop to tie your shoelace in Tollinghill and there'd be an elderly woman peering out of her window, wanting to know what you were doing. Then again, Ellis supposed that Hardwick would pull his usual 'DI Kempston Hardwick' stunt. Veronica's neighbours would be well aware of what had happened to her, so two men entering the house wouldn't look entirely out of place right now.

Veronica's cottage was tastefully decorated, but not cluttered. There were a few ornaments and pieces of furniture he was sure must have come from one of Tollinghill's many antique shops, but they'd clearly been carefully chosen by someone with a keen eye for interior design. That was something Ellis wished he had. Alas, he had enough trouble matching trousers with shirts.

Eventually, they found the room Veronica had used as her study. It was styled in the same way as the rest of the cottage, with tasteful antique furniture and a gorgeous old dark wooden desk, on which sat a very modern-looking Apple iMac. Then again, Ellis supposed, those probably didn't come in a waxed cherry finish.

'You'd have thought the police would have taken that,' Ellis said, pointing at the computer. 'To search for evidence. Clues and stuff.'

'The world is changing, Ellis,' Hardwick said. 'They can clone machines rather efficiently nowadays. It only takes a few minutes to completely mirror the machine. Then it can be left where it was found and the police can take their time in searching the clone for anything of interest.'

Ellis raised his eyebrows and let out a small murmur of surprise. He had enough trouble starting up his own computer, without worrying about in-depth computer forensics.

Compared to Hardwick, Veronica Campbell's priorities had clearly veered towards the functional, he thought, as he noticed a collection of Bic pens in a pot on her desk, alongside a diary and a couple of notebooks he recognised from the shelves at the local supermarket.

Everything about the layout and setup of the study gave off a sense of efficiency and organisation — far removed from the impression her ex-husband gave of her having spiralled into a pit of depression and alcoholism. Then again, perhaps her way of coping was to completely separate her professional and social lives.

Maybe this was her sanctuary, the place where she maintained her capable and competent side, diligently taking care of Rupert Pearson's public relations and engagements.

He supposed it was the only way Pearson would have kept employing her. After all, the author didn't seem like the sort of person who'd put up with anything less than a professional job.

Hardwick picked up Veronica's diary and began to flick through it. It seemed she used it for both work and personal purposes, with a combination of Rupert Pearson's engagements and her own private appointments listed.

He looked at a couple of the pages more closely than the others and pursed his lips.

Ellis knew this tended to mean he'd spotted something of interest. 'What is it?' he asked.

'This entry here. The day before she was murdered. It says "Evelyn".'

'And? Maybe she had a meeting with someone called Evelyn.'

Hardwick shook his head. 'No. Look at the other entries. Every time she had a meeting with someone, she wrote it out in full. *Meeting with Jason Plumley at Alessandro's. Meeting with Julia Harshall at Noveco offices.* I thought at first maybe it was a friend she had coming over, but look back here, a few weeks earlier. *Peter visiting. Lara coming to stay.* She never deviated from the full form. Ever. Except the day before she was murdered, when she just wrote "Evelyn".

'Maybe she was in a hurry,' Ellis offered.

'No. It doesn't quite work like that, Ellis. People don't deviate that heavily just because they're in a rush. In any case, look how neatly the word is written. That was not a fast-moving pen. Have no doubt that Veronica Campbell was in no particular hurry when she wrote that word.'

'So she wrote someone's name down. It still doesn't tell us anything.'

'On the contrary, Ellis. Deviation from known behaviours tells us an awful lot. In most cases, this is exactly what the police look for in their suspects. Any change in behaviour tends to be viewed as highly suspicious.'

'What, so you think Veronica killed herself?'

'Not for one moment, Ellis. But I think there was far more going on than meets the eye.'

18

Like many British men, Kempston Hardwick tended to find he was better at thinking about things after a drink or two. He wasn't sure whether the alcohol itself gave him any specific cognitive advantage or whether it was entirely psychosomatic in the same way stroking one's beard aided logical conclusions. But, not being the sort of man who'd entertain the idea of facial hair, Hardwick would have to make do with a drink.

He and Ellis walked from Veronica Campbell's cottage with a spring in their step and a weight on their shoulders. They certainly felt as though they'd discovered something of importance, but at the same time they weren't entirely sure what it was or how they could identify the elusive Evelyn.

'It might be worth speaking to her ex-husband again. He might know who Evelyn is,' Ellis offered.

'No,' Hardwick replied. 'I can tell you now he won't know who she is. There's a reason Veronica wrote the name down on its own, without any context. It's something she wanted to keep to herself, and wouldn't even reveal in her own diary. I think it's very unlikely *anyone* will know who Evelyn is.'

'Someone must know, surely.'

'Someone will, of course. But until we know more, I don't think it's wise we go asking around. We wouldn't want to spook anyone, particularly if this Evelyn was a sensitive subject for Veronica or, even worse, was what caused somebody to murder her.'

'That's all well and good, Kempston, but there aren't even any suspects. Apart from Terry Cox, that is.'

Hardwick gave Ellis a look which told him not to go there. 'There will be suspects, Ellis. Don't you worry. These things have to be done in a logical order. The first suspect is always the lover or partner. In this case, Terry Cox. The less said about that, the better. The second port of call is the ex-husband, but David Campbell was in London with a large number of people on the night Veronica was murdered. Then there's her employer, Rupert Pearson. He was at the book launch with us, waiting for Veronica at the time she was murdered. Most murder victims are killed by someone close to them, but it seems this might be one of those rare occurrences where we have to cast our net a little wider.'

'She had a sister, though,' Ellis said, as if this was common knowledge.

Hardwick stopped walking. 'Since when?'

Ellis shrugged. 'Since whenever the youngest one of them was born, I suppose.'

'How long have you known about this? You never mentioned a word.'

'Dougie told me. I didn't think it was relevant.'

'You didn't think it was relevant?' Hardwick said, turning on him. 'The vast, overwhelming majority of murder victims are killed by a friend or family member and you didn't think it was relevant to tell me Veronica Campbell had a sister?'

'Well it's hardly likely to be her, is it? She doesn't even live locally, from what Dougie was saying. Somewhere in London, apparently.'

Hardwick looked at Ellis for a moment, then marched off down the road towards the Freemason's Arms.

---

Ellis finally caught up with Hardwick just as he entered

the pub. He'd gradually come to realise why Hardwick didn't own a car. It wasn't due to environmental concerns or wanting to save money: it was because he could walk at twice the speed limit of most roads.

By the time Ellis had got his breath back, Hardwick had already convinced the barmaid to summon Doug down from upstairs.

'Veronica Campbell's sister,' Hardwick said to Doug, without even saying hello. 'Do you know her name or where she lives?'

'Her sister?'

'Yes.'

'I think I do, actually,' Doug said after a moment. 'Veronica wanted to get her a particular bottle of gin for her birthday a few months back, and asked me if I could get it for her. There's a company I use for specialist drinks and stuff, see. She gave me the address and I got them to send it straight on to her.'

'And do you still have it?'

'Well, yeah. I have the email I sent to the company.'

Hardwick stood and stared at Doug.

'Oh, you want me to get it?' the landlord asked, eventually.

'Please.'

A couple of minutes later, he came back downstairs

with his laptop and jabbed at a few buttons on the keyboard.

'Takes ages, this bloody connection. If you ask me, they need to roll out that superfibre broadnet thing a bit quicker. Ah, here we go. Want me to write it down?'

Hardwick snatched the laptop and turned it round to face him. 'No, that'll be fine,' he said, glancing at the screen and turning on his heels. 'Thank you!'

Ellis gave chase, breaking into a sprint in order to keep up with Hardwick.

'You can't go being rude to people who are trying to help you, Kempston,' he said, when he finally caught up.

'I wasn't being rude, Ellis. I was being efficient. Besides which, I said thank you.'

'Sometimes it takes a bit more than that.'

'Well maybe I'll buy him a box of chocolates on my way back. I really don't have the time or capacity for this sort of nonsense.'

'Where are you going anyway?'

'To the station, Ellis. We're going to visit Veronica Campbell's sister.'

'We? But I've got my dinner in half an hour.'

'You're more than welcome to stay here if you'd prefer. I'm quite comfortable being on my own.'

Ellis jogged alongside Hardwick, glancing between

his watch, his friend and the fast-disappearing sight of Tollinghill behind them.

'Where does she even live?'

'Tooting. Thirty-nine Hallmark Way. We'll be there in under two hours.'

'Two hours?!'

'There's no time like the present. Like I said, Ellis. You're more than welcome to stay here.'

It really shouldn't be a tough decision when being asked to choose between spending four hours on a train with a man with no social skills, or a cosy night in watching TV. But, for Ellis, curiosity and intrigue often won out. And, if he was just a little bit honest with himself, there was a large part of him that was still the six-year-old Ellis Flint who was enthralled by detective fiction and thrived on the chance of discovering the killer before the detective.

Although this was far from fiction. This was real-life murder.

19

Although they'd had to change trains once they arrived in London, both trains were national rail services and Hardwick had bought both himself and Ellis first-class tickets.

Many people thought Hardwick to be snobbish or stuck-up, but Ellis knew him well enough to know that was not the case. In fact, he'd be hard pushed to think of another person who was more concerned with social justice than Kempston Hardwick.

The truth was that Hardwick was not someone who judged anyone by class, background or wealth. But he had his own set of standards by which society generally failed to live.

Ellis got the impression that Hardwick thought the world would be a much better place if people could just be nice to each other. He seemed to have a burning desire for justice and stamping out unfairness wherever he saw it. And it was true to say that there were a lot of things he didn't like or looked down his nose at. But Ellis knew that wasn't strictly snobbery. Kempston Hardwick just knew what he liked — and what he didn't like. And, if Ellis had to be honest with himself, he'd actually become quite fond of the old git.

Having snored loudly for most of the journey, he now found himself with a dry throat and a sore arm from where Hardwick had poked him with a pen as the train pulled into their station. By now, it was early evening and Ellis had been grateful for the first-class tickets. Even their carriage was starting to get full, swelled with the commuters on their way back to the suburbs, who'd use their overpriced house as a hotel room before shuffling lifelessly towards the station again at the crack of dawn.

It would be fair to say that Tooting was a busier place than Tollinghill. As one of south London's busiest boroughs, the main road was bustling with commuters and locals, and the whole place felt alive with colour and vibrancy. It was an almost alien environment for Ellis, who hadn't been to London in many years. He supposed it could have been as many as eight, when the pair had come to speak to somebody about another murder.

Ellis quietly took stock of this sobering thought: that his only visits to the capital, which was practically on his doorstep, were not for relaxing nights out at the theatre but to investigate grisly deaths. He sometimes wondered how different his life might have been if he hadn't struck up conversation with Kempston Hardwick that night eight years earlier.

Veronica's sister lived only a short walk from the station, although everything was a short walk when Hardwick was setting the pace. It occurred to Ellis, as he jogged to keep up with him, that he still didn't know what Veronica's sister's name was. And he didn't find out until a couple of minutes later when the doorbell was answered by a dark-haired woman who very much gave off the air of a suburban Londoner.

'Olivia Nicholson?' Hardwick said, again miraculously making himself sound like a police officer.

Olivia sighed and opened the door a little further. 'Yes, come in,' she said.

A little perplexed, but not about to refuse the offer, the pair entered the smart Georgian terrace house.

'Sorry, I didn't mean to sound rude,' she said, closing the door behind them. 'It's been a dreadful few days, as you can imagine. It's just they said you'd be popping by tomorrow morning.'

'Ah. Yes. Well, there's been a slight change of plan,

I'm afraid. Must be a mix-up back at the office,' Hardwick replied.

Olivia forced a smile and led them through to the
large kitchen at the back of the house, which appeared to
go on for miles. Although it looked tall and thin from the
front, the inside was more like the Tardis than a terraced
house.

'I've picked out a couple of songs I know she used to
love. I presume David will have given you some
suggestions too, so I don't know which ones you think are
best to use. I don't suppose it really matters too much.'

It was at this point that it began to dawn on Hardwick that Olivia hadn't mistaken them for police officers.

'Ah. I think there might have been a misunderstand-
ing,' he said. 'We're actually here to ask a few questions
about Veronica, regarding our investigation into her
death.'

Olivia stopped what she was doing and looked at the
pair of them. 'Oh. You mean you're not the funeral
directors?'

'No, we're not.'

'Oh. It's just that... you know. Looking like that,' she
said, gesturing to Hardwick. 'And there's always a short
dumpy one, isn't there?'

Hardwick glanced at Ellis, who had the face of a
startled rabbit.

'Indeed so. Alas, we are not funeral directors. Would you mind if we were to ask you a few questions? We promise we won't take up too much of your time.'

Olivia sighed again, more deeply this time. 'Alright. I guess it gives me something else to do other than moping round the house. Although I don't know what else I can tell you. I told your colleagues our whole bloody life story. Everything from the moment I was born. Three and a half hours they were here. I was on the verge of asking them if I was legally obliged to provide a rent book.'

Hardwick smiled graciously. 'So you're the youngest sister, are you?'

'Yes. Oldest and youngest now, I suppose. An only child. Although I'm not a child, of course. Then again, it doesn't stop me being an orphan either. Or does it? When do people stop using that word?'

Hardwick decided it would be best not to directly address Olivia's question, which in any case he hoped was rhetorical.

'Did you see your sister often?' he asked.

Olivia looked sadder for a moment. 'Not often enough, probably. But life somehow manages to get in the way, doesn't it?'

Hardwick had heard this story many times before. 'Indeed. When did you see her last?'

'I was thinking about this the other day. I think it must have been just before Christmas. She was visiting an old uni friend in Surrey and we met up for lunch on her way back.'

'And how did she seem?'

'Well she didn't appear to have any premonition that she was going to get murdered in a few months, if that's what you mean.'

'Not quite what I meant, no. I mean had she changed at all? Was she the same sort of person you always knew?'

Olivia swallowed and looked away. 'She'd changed since she and David split up, obviously. But then again marriage breakups do that to people.'

'Changed in what way?'

'She was.... I don't know. Different. It was almost as if all the things she'd had to hold back during her marriage were just spilling out. Almost like a sort of mid-life crisis. She did a pretty good job of trying to hide it with me, but she couldn't hide it from the people closest to her.'

Hardwick nodded. 'And how do you know that?'

Olivia looked up at him slowly, registering his meaning and realising that he'd probably already suspected the answer. She took a deep breath before answering.

'David told me a few of the things she'd said and done.'

'Do you see him often?'

'Occasionally. He works in London quite a lot. Just round the corner from where I work. We sometimes meet for drinks after work.'

'Just drinks?'

Olivia looked at him. 'You're a grown man, Inspector. You know how these things work.'

Hardwick thought it would be easier to ignore the question than to answer it honestly.

'And when did this all start? Before or after your sister and her husband separated?'

'Nothing "started" as such. It was just a casual sort of thing, every now and again. And there wasn't exactly a date and time when they separated. It just sort of happened gradually over time. I think they'd been growing apart for a while.'

Hardwick and Ellis exchanged glances. Too often, they'd discovered some form of love triangle at the centre of a murder investigation, and it never surprised them to find one.

'You probably think I'm some sort of home wrecker,' Olivia said, before either Hardwick or Flint had said a word. 'But it wasn't like that. It's not the sort of thing I can explain easily, but Veronica and David had drifted apart a long time before anyone really knew about it.'

'And did Veronica know about you and David?' Hardwick asked.

'Honestly? I don't know. Not that she ever let on to me, anyway. But then again she wouldn't have done. She kept a lot of things to herself. I think that's probably half the reason she went off the rails a little bit.'

'Surely she would've mentioned if she'd found out her husband and sister were having an affair?' Ellis asked.

'It wasn't an *affair*,' Olivia replied, with an intonation that made it sound like he'd just accused her of shopping at Asda. 'And you didn't know Veronica. She was a brooder. She worked in PR, don't forget. It was natural for her to keep quiet and plan ahead.'

'Were you close?' Hardwick asked.

Olivia seemed to consider this for a moment before speaking. 'Not particularly. I'd like to say we were, but we were very different people. In many ways.'

'How so?'

Olivia swallowed and blinked a few times. 'I really don't feel comfortable. When your colleagues came, I... Well, it doesn't seem right saying things about people after they're gone, does it?'

'Was there something you wanted to tell them but didn't?' Hardwick asked.

Ellis knew better than most how poor his friend's social skills were, but there was no way he could fault his perception and intuition.

Olivia blinked again, then nodded. 'She had a dark side. All people do, I guess, but I always wondered if hers might get her into trouble one day.'

This certainly had the pair's attention. 'What sort of trouble?' Hardwick asked.

'When we were at school,' Olivia said, seemingly in her own dreamworld, 'there was an incident.'

'What sort of incident?'

'She's always been able to twist people round her little finger. Especially men. She's manipulative. She knows what she wants and she makes damn sure she's going to get it.'

Present tense, Hardwick noted. Psychologically interesting.

'There was a teacher. One she didn't like. A guy called Mr Chambers. He was probably only in his mid to late twenties himself. Veronica was, what, fourteen? Fifteen maybe? She hated him. All because he'd worked her out and knew what she was like. He was always one step ahead. He never fell for any of her tricks. Except one.'

'And what was that?'

'She made an accusation. Claimed he'd sexually assaulted her. Touched her up.'

'An unfounded allegation, presumably?' Hardwick said.

'Oh yes. Completely. Not a grain of truth in it.'

'Why would she do that?' Ellis asked.

'Because she needed to be in control. She needed to feel powerful. She had that with pretty much everyone else in her life. Certainly with our parents. But with Mr Chambers, he'd worked her out right from the beginning. He was totally in control, always knew where things were headed and how to deal with her. But he didn't spot that coming.'

'What happened to him?'

'He lost his job. Never taught again, so I hear. Back then, these sorts of stories were all over the media so he never stood a chance of getting another job in teaching.'

'All because of the say-so of one person?' Ellis asked.

'Sometimes that's all it takes. Especially when that one person manages to twist the police and social workers round their little finger, too. She knew exactly what she was doing. Her so-called friends backed her up, too. Well, we never really got to the bottom of that. I suspect she went running to them and told them Mr Chambers had done all this stuff. She could really turn on the waterworks when she wanted to. She'd have made a good actress. I was too young at the time, so my parents kind of shielded me from the detail. But from what I gather — or suspect — it was her friends who convinced her to report him and get something done about it. That gave it a lot of weight. The fact that she didn't just go crying to the authorities, but had to apparently be convinced to report it.'

'Clever,' Ellis said.

'There's a lot more to it nowadays, I understand. But that's how it was then. It just happened to be in that perfect gap, after the days when abuse was ignored or brushed off as "men being men", when people knew it was wrong and started to speak up, but the system hadn't yet caught up in terms of verifying claims.'

Hardwick had been watching Olivia carefully as she spoke, and had been struck by her manner and demeanour. She was clearly an intelligent woman, one who spoke articulately and had enjoyed a good education and career. But, underneath it all, was a scarred soul — the inner core of a young girl who'd grown up in the shadow of an older sister who, it seemed, had a destructive and controlling personality.

'And do you think she still had that side to her?' Ellis asked. 'Do you reckon she might have tried getting one over on the wrong people this time?'

Olivia shrugged. 'It's possible. You never really knew what she was going to do. Only she knew. She set her sights on something, and she did it. She didn't care who she trampled over on the way. That's just the way she was. If she could destroy someone else just to make herself look better, she would.'

'Blimey. I thought siblings were meant to get along and look out for each other.'

Olivia let out a noise that sounded like a horse with a bit of straw stuck up its nose.

'Normal siblings, maybe. But only if they're both decent people and one of them isn't willing to trample over the other for their own gain.'

Hardwick glanced at Ellis. Did he detect some sort of personal slight?

Ellis, though, darted into the silence with a question of his own.

'You go by the name Nicholson,' he asked. 'But you're not married, are you?'

Olivia shook her head. 'No. It's the name I was brought up with. My birth father left while Mum was pregnant with me. Veronica was only eighteen months old at the time and he couldn't handle the way his life had changed, so when he found out they were having a second inconvenient baby he disappeared. Why would I want to use his name?'

'And Nicholson was the name of your step-father?' Ellis asked.

'Yes. He was far from perfect, but at least he stuck around. For a while.'

'Far from perfect in what way?'

Olivia let out a sigh. 'He drunk a little bit too much sometimes. Was late home. Nothing too out of the ordinary.'

'Would you say "abusive alcoholic"?'

Olivia's face dropped. 'No. I wouldn't. But I know damn well who would. Veronica always had this romantic idea that our dad would just come waltzing back into our lives, because it had all been a terrible mistake and he'd just had a bump on the head which made him walk away and leave us on our own. It was absolutely insane. She never accepted Brian. Our step-dad. That was her all over, though. She had to make the decisions. She had to be in control.'

'Did she ever do anything directly to you?' Hardwick asked, taking the conversation back to Veronica's controlling and domineering nature.

'That all depends what you mean by "directly", doesn't it?' Olivia said. 'If you mean do I have an example of when she shafted me for her own gain, probably not, no. It sounds so silly, but it's little things like the fact that her behaviour and ways meant that all my parents' time was spent on dealing with her. I practically brought myself up. Even when I went through the same school a few years after her, the teachers would almost handle me with gloves on. It was as if I was just a smaller clone of her, as if I was going to do the same as she did. So yes, maybe there was a part of me that felt like I was getting one over on her by sleeping with David. Who knows? Maybe that was part of the attraction in the first place. But regardless of how cold and callous she was as a person, no-one wants to see their sister dead, do they?'

Hardwick looked at her and smiled, secretly hoping she was right.

20

Their return trip from London had been a quiet one. Their carriage on the train was completely empty apart from the two of them and a man sitting at the far end of the carriage reading a battered copy of the *Evening Standard* left on the table by a previous occupant.

Ellis noted the headline, decrying the mayor's plans to shut off certain roads in the city and make them dedicated cycle routes. He was nowhere near being able to read the text of the article from where he was sitting, but he'd have a good guess that the paper would be predicting a huge increase in city traffic whilst at the same time forecasting a fall in earnings for taxi drivers. 'Londoners aghast' the headline began, although Ellis doubted very much that was the case. It took quite a lot to rattle a Londoner, and cycle routes were unlikely to be high up the list.

The darkness outside served only to make Ellis feel even more tired than he already was. It was physically and mentally taxing enough spending his days with Kempston Hardwick, without having to take the grave-yard train back from south London after a day's antics.

He turned his head slightly towards his friend, who was, as always, sitting bolt upright and looking out of the window as if admiring the rolling hills and valleys. Ellis knew this couldn't be the case, though. Hardwick was a man of many talents, but infrared vision was not one of them.

It was clear to Ellis that Hardwick was taking part in his favourite hobby: thinking. Ellis Flint, on the other hand, actively tried not to think. There was no fun in it, he found.

He'd often wondered about Hardwick's background, and how despite the number of impossible crimes they'd managed to solve together, the biggest mystery of all was Hardwick himself. Even when Ellis did manage to find something out about him, it opened up a whole new avenue of mystery.

For instance, finding out that Kempston was his middle name, and that introducing himself as 'DI Kemp-ston Hardwick' when the occasion suited was not technically incorrect, his first two names being Dagwood Isambard. A reveal, a discovery, a new nugget of truth. But all that did was make Ellis wonder about the sort of parents who'd call their newborn baby Dagwood Isambard Kempston. The bullying at school must have been bad enough as it was, without the other students spotting those unfortunate initials.

Then again, Ellis wasn't one to comment on unusual forenames. His mother had been a radical feminist in the liberated 1960s, and amongst other passionate views on social justice she was convinced that Ruth Ellis, the last woman hanged in Britain, had been stitched up by the Establishment and should not have been executed. She'd felt so passionately about this she decided to name her firstborn after her martyred heroine, although she'd stopped just short of naming her son Ruth.

His mother had mellowed a little as she got older, but she'd always carried a torch for fighting social injustice. Ellis often wondered how much of his mother he saw in Kempston Hardwick. There were definite similarities, reminders. Although he couldn't quite imagine Kempston Hardwick burning a bra.

In fact, he knew absolutely nothing of Hardwick's childhood, other than the fact that his parents had clearly been under the influence of some sort of narcotic when naming him. Ellis remembered him mentioning some years back a childhood filled with travel. The way Hardwick said it made him think it wasn't just a lot of holidays.

Either way, Hardwick had either been brought up to keep things to himself and be a private sort of person, or something had happened to him to make him that way. To any outsider, it might seem easy or, indeed, logical to just come out and ask him about his background. But that wouldn't work with Hardwick. He was a master at shutting down a conversation and getting his own way. Many might have called it stubbornness or arrogance, but Ellis had seen another angle on it from early on. Kempston Hardwick was a man who knew the right way things should be, and he focused all his efforts on making sure it was so. Anything external was purely a distraction.

By anyone's standards, it was a bizarre set of circumstances. By rights, they weren't the sort of people who should ever become friends — not that Hardwick would ever come close to admitting that he considered anybody to be a friend. They were chalk and cheese, but in many ways that was an advantage.

Ellis's life had been a series of fortunate accidents, even as far back as his conception. Somehow, he always managed to be in the right place at the right time, and on more than one occasion his seemingly random and inane mutterings had led them directly to a murderer. Ellis, of course, maintained it was entirely deliberate on each occasion and took every opportunity to let Hardwick know that. But he recognised that without Hardwick seeing the relevance in what he was saying, it was unlikely he'd have ever come close to solving a crime. And, in his heart of hearts, he suspected Hardwick knew he'd come to rely on Ellis's 'outside the box' thinking, much as he'd never admit it.

When push came to shove, it really didn't matter who got or took the plaudits. More often than not, it was the police who got the credit anyway. To Ellis, it didn't matter much. He was just having plenty of fun and getting out of the house for a bit. For Hardwick, it sated his desire for justice and eradicating inequality.

And, after all, justice is what it was all about, wasn't it?

21

By now, Hardwick had become thoroughly frustrated. He was used to people not wanting to talk to him or keeping things to themselves, but that wasn't what was happening here. This was something else entirely. This was a case of people being perfectly honest and open with him, but still not getting anywhere near the truth.

Any less stubborn person would have started to wonder if perhaps Terry Cox *was* guilty of Veronica Campbell's murder. But Hardwick had never wavered from his convictions at any point in his life, and he wasn't about to start now.

He had a knack for knowing when things weren't quite right, almost a sixth sense for disorder and the pattern of life being knocked slightly out of kilter. It was almost like walking into a room and noticing one of the pictures on the wall being slightly skew-whiff. It might take a moment to work out in which direction it needed adjusting, but there'd be no doubt it wasn't quite right.

That was life for Kempston Hardwick: overly perceptive to the point of sometimes missing the basics.

He'd been known to overanalyse situations and people at the expense of a more fundamental clue, and on one or two occasions had felt cause to blame himself for killers not being caught sooner. Usually, though, it was the deception and duplicity of others which delayed cases, and in those situations he was even more fired up to identify and locate the killer.

Sometimes, it was a case of casting his net a little wider. He'd often been surprised at where the most valuable clues had come from.

That was why he'd waited a little further along the road from Rupert Pearson's house that next morning, and waited for him to get in his car and drive to the train station.

He'd discovered Pearson would be attending an event in London that day, and that his attendance had been confirmed despite the recent loss of his PA. Hardwick admired Pearson's professionalism and stoicism, and silently thanked him for getting out of the way for a few hours.

He gave it a few minutes, then stepped out ready to

walk up towards Pearson's house, when he felt a hand on his shoulder.

'Alright, Kempston?' Ellis said, beaming from ear to ear. 'How's it hanging?'

Not quite sure how to answer this question, Hardwick instead asked one of his own. 'What are you doing here, Ellis?'

'Come out for a walk. Lovely morning, isn't it?'

'It was, yes.'

'Where are you off to?'

'I was going to speak to Rupert Pearson's wife.'

'Well, don't let me stop you.'

'I won't.'

'Can I come with?'

Hardwick let out a sigh. 'Is there any point in me saying "no"?'

The pair walked up to Pearson's house and knocked on the door. Thirty seconds or so later, a woman answered — a woman Hardwick presumed must be who he was looking for.

'Mrs Pearson?' Hardwick asked, not knowing what she looked like, but having discovered a brief, passing mention of Pearson's wife in a magazine article from a year or two earlier.

'Yes,' the woman replied, her voice gentle and smooth. Her hair was cut short and was light in colour.

The only thing Hardwick knew about her was that she and Rupert Pearson had been married only two or three years, but he was starting to pick up more already: like the impression that Mrs Pearson was a wise woman who'd seen the ways of the world.

'DI Kempston Hardwick,' came the reply. 'Can we have a quick chat?'

'That depends. What's it about?'

'Veronica Campbell.'

The woman nodded, and let them in. 'I thought Rupert had already told you everything he knew?'

'Yes,' Hardwick said, making his way through to the living room, 'but we have to speak to everybody in turn. It's surprising what can be missed, or what people presume others know or have said. Just one of those routine things, I'm afraid.'

By now, Mrs Pearson had entered the living room too.

'I've just put the kettle on if you want a cup.'

Hardwick raised a hand. 'No thank you, Mrs Pearson. We'd best get on so we can leave you in peace.'

Mrs Pearson gestured towards a leather chesterfield sofa. 'Cathy, by the way.'

Hardwick forced another smile. To him, using somebody's forename only minutes after meeting them was akin to walking into their house naked.

'So how well did you know Veronica Campbell?'

Cathy Pearson let out a sigh. 'I don't know, really. Pretty well, I think. She used to spend a fair bit of time round here, working with Rupert on things. She used to come round at least once a week, if not more, to brief him on upcoming media appearances, plans for future book launches, things like that. He used to keep her up to speed with how his work in progress was going, and she'd work out the best way to publicise things.'

'Were you friendly on a social level?' Hardwick asked.

'We were, but not so much recently. When she was still with her husband, David, they came over occasionally for dinner and drinks, but it wasn't long before they separated and all that stopped.'

'Veronica had been working with Rupert for some time, though, hadn't she? Have you and he not been together long?'

'We've been married just under three years,' Cathy replied. 'We only met five months prior to that. One of those "love in later life" stories, I suppose.'

'Were you married before?'

'I was. Twice. My second husband died from a sudden heart attack about two years before I met Rupert.'

'And your first?'

Cathy Pearson seemed disappointed to have been asked this. 'Is it really relevant?'

'Just context,' Hardwick replied.

'I was nineteen, he was an abusive bully, my father was a divorce lawyer. You can probably figure the rest out for yourself.'

Hardwick decided now might be a good time to change the conversation ever so slightly.

'After Veronica and David Campbell separated, did you notice any changes in her behaviour?'

'Well, I'll be honest with you, I don't really get out much. I'm not exactly one of the town gossips. But Rupert mentioned she was seeing some new chap. She started to come round less often. She'd cancel or postpone and say she was ill, even though I can't remember her being ill once before then. If you ask me, I'd put my money on a hangover. There were a couple of times she came over to talk Rupert through something and she stank of booze. Said she'd been at a lunch meeting with someone. Not particularly professional, but Rupert had worked with her for a long time and he trusted her. She was still good at her job, and it'd be very difficult to replace her. No-one knew his books like she did, and would have been impossible for him to show someone new the ropes.'

Hardwick nodded. 'Has he mentioned what he's going to do moving forward?'

'No. Not really. To be honest, he's still in shock. He's getting on with things as best he can, but that's Rupert for you. His oldest friend died last year. He was best man at our wedding. They'd been thick as thieves since school. When he heard the news he looked shellshocked, then decided to go and write a couple of chapters of his next novel. It's his way of coping. I couldn't do it, personally. I don't know how anyone can write a book with that much on their mind.'

'Has he spoken much to you about Veronica's death?' Hardwick asked.

'No, he's not really a talker. Dangerous world nowadays, isn't it? This is why I don't go out walking at night. Mind you, I'm usually tucked up by nine o'clock. That's what years of early starts does for you. Rupert's never one to talk about how he feels, though. Maybe it'll come through in one of his books, in some way. That's how he tends to deal with things. He'll fictionalise them and explore them through his characters. I guess that's how he tries to make sense of things. It's the only way he knows how.'

After a few more fairly innocuous questions, the pair stood and went to leave. As they reached the door, Hardwick stopped and turned back towards Cathy Pearson, asking her one more question as if it had been an afterthought rather than the whole reason he'd come to see her.

'I almost forgot. Does the name Evelyn mean anything to you?'

'Evelyn?' Sandra replied, furrowing her brow before shaking her head. 'I don't think I know anyone by that name. Why's that?'

Hardwick smiled. 'No reason. Thank you for your time, Mrs Pearson.'

Ellis chased Hardwick up the road and eventually caught up with him.

'Nice one. Now she'll think her husband was having an affair.'

'It's none of my concern what people think, Ellis. And, in any case, who's to say he wasn't? We still don't know who Evelyn is, so it's perfectly reasonable to assume there might be some nefarious connection.'

'She might be lying. Mrs Pearson, I mean.'

'She might. But I don't think so. I can say with almost complete certainty that Mrs Pearson was not lying.'

'Saw it in her eyes, did you?' Ellis asked, perhaps a little facetiously.

'Yes, Ellis, I did. And her mouth, ears, nose and in every single part of her body. I do hope the idea of understanding and interpreting body language is not alien to you.'

'Far from it,' Ellis said, almost to himself. 'Par for the course, hanging round with you.'

'I've never had any difficulty telling if someone's lying, Ellis. That's the easy bit. The difficulty is in finding out *why* they're lying, who or what they're protecting and what the truth actually is. Knowing someone is lying is only as useful as knowing your central heating has stopped working. The fault still requires diagnosis and repair. But, at the very least, one should start by looking at the boiler.'

Ellis wondered if perhaps he was trying to read too much into that comment, but quickly decided it might just be easier to give up and ignore it.

22

Ellis often had trouble keeping track of what day it was, but he always knew it was Saturday when Mrs F sat in front of the TV, enthusiastically watching her favourite dance reality show.

That was Ellis's computer night. He'd often get deliberately lost down the rabbit warren of Wikipedia or, if he fancied something a little lighter, he'd watch videos of car crashes on YouTube.

This week, his mind was elsewhere and, try as he might, he really couldn't focus on the article about the assassination of Archduke Franz Ferdinand. When the video of the Nissan Micra being t-boned by an eighteen-ton artic failed to capture his attention either, he turned his online efforts towards the thing that had been consuming his brain cells all evening, and long before: the small issue of the mysterious cottage.

That Rupert Pearson had, on at least one occasion, visited a particular cottage in Tollinghill wasn't in or of itself remarkable. But something about it, and him, had felt extremely out of place.

Up until now, Ellis had tried not to think too far into it, especially as he was so often keen to rebuke Hardwick for relying on gut feeling or intuition. But there was no denying that Ellis was convinced something wasn't right.

Fortunately for him, he'd had a bit of a brainwave. Feeling very proud of himself (but also a little worried) he went to the Land Registry website.

HM Land Registry was, he knew, where documents on home ownership — as well as the associated deeds — were kept in the UK. They were the ultimate arbiters when it came to boundary disputes and issues of ownership. To his joy, the homepage offered him an option labelled 'Search property ownership information'.

He clicked the link and was taken to a search page, where he was asked to enter the property name or number along with its postcode.

Ellis cursed at himself. Although he knew the number, he had no idea what the postcode was. He was only fairly sure he knew what his own postcode was.

Unfazed, he opened Google and typed in the street

name and 'Tollinghill', and hit enter. A resident of the same road appeared to run a business consultancy firm, whose website proudly displayed the full address — and postcode.

Ellis went back to the Land Registry website and entered this new piece of information, then hit Search. He was presented with three options: the title register, title plan and Flood Risk Indicator result — each of which cost three pounds.

He fumbled around for his wallet — which he was sure was here somewhere — and thought about which option he needed to order. He had no idea what the difference was between a title register and a title plan, so ordered both, sagely assuming that the Flood Risk Indicator result wouldn't be much use to him.

In the end, it was the title register he wanted, and the information was there in black and white. The cottage Rupert Pearson had been seen going into was owned by a company called Aspire Creative Solutions. Although Ellis knew what all three of those words meant, he couldn't make head nor tail of their meaning when put together. And, in any case, it really wound him up when companies mentioned 'solutions' at every given opportunity.

Keen to find out more, he nipped over to the Companies House website and searched for Aspire Creative

Solutions. The company's registered office was in London — a faceless mail-only address, Ellis presumed. He clicked the People tab, which would tell him the list of company directors.

When he did so, he found only one.

The company's sole director was listed as Rupert Arthur Pearson.

23

Ellis had, of course, immediately called Hardwick to tell him what he'd discovered. Hardwick insisted they spring into action, but Ellis was hesitant. His thinking on that was twofold: he wanted Hardwick to sleep on the information, and in any case it was far too late to start marching round to Rupert Pearson's house.

Hardwick was steadfast, though. After all, they knew Pearson's wife went to bed early and would be out of the way by now. He told Ellis he was going to see Pearson whether Ellis liked it or not, and had given him an ultimatum: was he coming or not? Ellis had, of course, said yes.

It soon became clear to the pair that Rupert Pearson wasn't the sort of person who often had visitors on a Saturday night, finally arriving at his front door in his dressing gown, a wine glass in one hand as he stifled a yawn with the other.

'Good evening, Mr Pearson,' Hardwick said, with an almost deliberate jollity. 'May we come in?'

It seemed to take Pearson a moment or two to work out who Hardwick was, but he stood aside nonetheless and let them inside.

'Shouldn't you be in the pub?' Pearson said, following them into the kitchen and clearly now recalling who Hardwick was. 'What sort of time do you call this?'

'Five to ten, Mr Pearson. No time like the present, is there?'

'There is if it's five to ten.'

The atmosphere was stained by the sound of Rupert Pearson's washing machine screeching and grinding in the corner. Pearson walked over and gave it a kick. 'Bloody thing. It really doesn't like me. If it was up to me we'd get a new one, but there we go. Clinging on for dear life, like the rest of us.'

'How did the thing in London go?' Ellis asked, trying to break the ice but not realising the idiocy of his words.

'Thing?'

'You went to an event today, didn't you?' By now, Ellis could see Hardwick gesticulating wildly behind Pearson, but was nowhere near being able to interpret it.

'Well, yes. How did you know about that?'

Quickly cottoning on to Hardwick's throat-slicing "don't tell him" motion, Ellis cleverly decided to lie.

'Uh, your wife told us.'

Hardwick closed his eyes and threw his head back.

'My wife? When?'

'Mmmm. That's a good question.'

'Wait a sec. You're not the two blokes who came round earlier, are you? She said it was two police officers.'

'Did she?' Hardwick said, guiding Pearson towards a kitchen chair. 'How very strange. Anyway, I'm sure it all went marvellously. Do you mind if we just ask you a couple of quick questions?'

'Well, that all depends on who's asking, doesn't it?'

'We are,' Ellis said, helpfully.

'As police officers or as blokes from the pub?'

'As people who have a couple of questions they'd like you to answer,' Hardwick said.

Pearson pushed his chair back and stood up. 'I think you two had better leave before I call the real police,' he said, reaching for his phone.

'Why does Aspire Creative Solutions own a cottage in Tollinghill, Mr Pearson?' Hardwick asked.

Pearson froze on the spot, and spoke without turning back to them.

'How did you know about that?' he replied, after a few moments. Hardwick could almost follow his train of thought, having considered denial but realising the pair hadn't just guessed this information.

'Research,' Hardwick replied, pulling a sheet of paper out of his inside jacket pocket before showing it briefly to Pearson. 'So do you want to tell us a little more about it, or do you want to call the "real" police?'

Pearson slowly turned and sat back down in the chair.

'Alright. Yes, the company owns property in the town. So what?'

'And you're the sole director of the company, are you not?'

'Yes. I am. It holds a number of assets, including that cottage.'

'Ah, so you know which one we're talking about, do you?'

Pearson looked at Hardwick, but didn't reply.

'What do you use the property for, Mr Pearson? Do you rent it out?'

'No,' Pearson said, quickly. 'Not at the moment, anyway. I use it for storage. Why, would you like a guided tour?'

Hardwick was tempted to say yes, but decided against it. Once again, he was sure his intuition was right, but he knew he needed to be careful how he proved it.

He was tempted — very tempted — to ask Pearson one more question. But that was a question that was best left for now.

24

'So you think he was lying to us?' Ellis asked, as they walked back down the hill from Rupert Pearson's house and into Tollinghill.

'Through his back teeth, Ellis. That cottage isn't used for storage any more than I'm a member of the Royal Ballet.'

'Christ, what I wouldn't pay to see that!'

'Don't worry, Ellis. There's not much chance of that happening. But we have to move quickly.'

'How do you mean?'

Hardwick had, as he often did, kept his ideas and theories largely to himself, waiting for the perfect opportunity to strike. And this, he was sure, was it.

'Rupert Pearson now knows we know about the cottage. You could see from his reaction it's not something he wanted anyone finding out about, so we need to move on to the next stage immediately, before he gets ahead of us.'

'And how do we do that?' Ellis asked.

'We go back to the cottage. We knock again. And this time, we don't take "no" for an answer.'

25

The night air was still as the pair walked cautiously up Park Road towards the junction with Elm Walk. Just before they got there, they turned into the alleyway and slowed their pace slightly as they approached the back gate to the cottage.

'Ready?' Hardwick asked, watching as Ellis's face betrayed signs of nervousness.

'No. I really think we should wait until the morning. Sleep on it, perhaps.'

'What, and give Pearson time to cover his tracks? No chance. We don't have that option any more, Ellis. We're going in.'

Before Ellis could protest, Hardwick had pushed open the back gate and was marching up the path towards the back of the cottage. When he got there, he paused for a moment before trying the handle. It yielded.

Silently, he pulled the handle down further and gave the door a slight push, allowing it to open into a dated but cosy kitchen.

Ellis followed him in, and Hardwick motioned for him to leave the door open, just in case they needed to leave the building quickly.

Although the cottage seemed pretty small from the outside, it seemed even tinier once they were inside it. The decor was dark and gloomy, and Hardwick noted that although the place was a little cluttered, there was no sign that anyone had been using it for any great level of storage.

From the kitchen, they rounded a tight archway and into the living room. Again, the room looked well lived-in and Hardwick got the strong impression this cottage was definitely used for residential means rather than storing Rupert Pearson's belongings.

He glanced at the pile of papers on the coffee table, nodding slowly to himself.

'There's no TV,' Ellis whispered. 'Who the hell has no TV?'

Hardwick decided not to answer, and instead headed towards the stairs.

He was sure they would creak underfoot, but they

didn't. This was clearly one of those older properties which was extremely well-built and hadn't yet fallen apart.

As they reached the top of the stairs, they realised there were only two rooms up here: a bedroom and a bathroom. Realising there was probably very little they could glean from the latter, Hardwick pushed open the door to the bedroom.

Although the room was gloomy, a shaft of light had cut through the curtains and cast itself on one end of the bed.

'Jesus Christ!' Ellis said, whispered but forceful.

Hardwick held up a finger to silence him. It was clear what they could both see.

In the bed lay a woman, old and pallid. Her skin was almost white, with a slight tinge of grey, and her hair looked like grey pondweed gripping a dry shovel.

'Is she dead?' Ellis whispered, looking at her chest for signs of breathing, but seeing none.

Hardwick stepped forward to take a closer look.

As he did so, the woman's eyes opened and locked straight onto his. Before he had a chance to say anything, a shrill, piercing scream rang through the room.

26

They had, of course, done as they were told when the old woman had screamed at them to get out. In fact, Ellis had never moved so fast and had almost kept up pace with Hardwick. Almost.

Like anyone being yelled at by a deranged person, Hardwick and Flint went straight to their safe haven — in their case, the pub.

Neither of them said a word until they were in the Freemason's Arms, which seemed an odd place to go in such a situation but, at the same time, perfectly natural.

'What the hell was all that about?' Ellis said, panting as they pointed at their respective pump clips, Hardwick having decided to forego his usual Campari and orange in favour of a low-percentage beer to quickly quench his thirst.

'I'm not entirely sure. But I think I've got an idea. We're nearly there, Ellis. There's just that last, gritty little bit. I can almost taste it.'

'That'll be the hops,' Doug said, appearing as if by magic. 'From New Zealand, apparently. Seven eighty please, lads.'

Ellis grabbed Hardwick's empty glass and put it, and his own, back down on the bar.

'Campari and orange and a Pheasant Plucker please, Dougie.'

Doug raised his eyebrows. 'You want to be careful saying things like that after chugging a pint. Here, do you want to try this whisky? Limited edition, it is.'

'Looks nice,' Ellis said. 'How much is it?'

'Forty-six quid for a single. But I can do you a double for ninety-eight.'

'Jesus Christ! That's expensive for a bottle, never mind a shot.'

'Limited edition, mate. Only a hundred bottles ever made.'

'I'll be alright thanks.'

With their bar tab — sans whisky — already now nearing twenty pounds from just the past thirty seconds or so, Hardwick paid for the drinks and the pair retired to a quiet table in the corner — almost exactly on the spot where just a few days earlier he'd been reading out a passage from Rupert Pearson's book. That all seemed a long time ago now. Their usual habit was to sit at the bar — Hardwick much preferring it as a spot for people-watching and observing the nuances of society — but this conversation was going to require some privacy.

'So do you think that's his bit on the side?' Ellis asked, having already downed half of his second pint.

Hardwick looked at him, waiting for the tell-tale giggle Ellis always did when he was telling a silly joke. After a few seconds, he realised he was serious.

'Ellis, I might not be the best person to comment on issues of love and romance, but I think we can quite safely assume that woman was not Rupert Pearson's mistress.'

'You never know. Takes all sorts.'

'Yes, but I'm not entirely sure there's such a thing as a fetish for ghosts.'

'She looked pretty bloomin' alive to me.'

'Oh, she was alive alright. She just didn't look it.'

'Certainly sounded it.'

'Yes. She wasn't particularly keen on our presence.'

'Probably thought we'd broken in, to be fair to her. We technically did, didn't we?'

'No, we trespassed. The door was unlocked, as was the gate, and we didn't force entry.'

'Oh, that's alright then,' Ellis said. 'I told you it was a bad idea.'

'Trespass isn't a criminal offence,' Hardwick replied.

'Neither's sticking your head in a boiling pot of water, but I'm not going to try it.'

The pair sat silently for a few moments before Ellis spoke again.

'You think you know who she is, don't you? You've got that glint in your eye.'

'I think I might be pretty close, yes,' Hardwick replied. 'I might still be wrong. I doubt it, but I might. Hand me your phone, Ellis.'

'My phone? Why?'

'So I can send a text message.'

Ellis narrowed his eyebrows as he looked at Hardwick. 'You never stop amazing me, Kempston. This is the man who still struggles with light switches.'

'I'm perfectly capable of sending a text message, Ellis.'

'So why don't you get your own phone?'

'Because I have no need for one. Now hand it over.'

'No need for one? You're constantly asking to use mine, for a start. That's usually a sign that you need something. When's your birthday? I'll buy you one.'

'You certainly will not,' Hardwick said, snatching the phone from Ellis's pocket, unlocking it, firing off a text message and deleting it before Ellis could stop him.

'Wait. How did you know the code to unlock my phone?' Ellis asked.

'Don't be ridiculous, Ellis. I've seen you enter that code a hundred times. I knew it from the first time.'

'You always know everything, don't you?' Ellis said. 'How long have you known who that woman in that cottage is?'

'Not long. A few things came together in my mind while we were in the cottage.'

'So why did you run?' Ellis asked.

'Why did you?'

'Because there was some half-dead mad woman screaming in my face!'

'Quite.'

'Do you think she's dangerous?'

'Not to us.'

Ellis looked at his friend, a curious look on his face. 'What do you mean by that?'

'Let's just see if I'm right first, shall we?'

Ellis laughed and shook his head. 'I think we both know you will be. I just don't know why you won't tell me. Why do you never tell me these things when you work them out?'

'Drama, Ellis. Besides which, I don't trust you any

further than I can throw you.' He drained the remains of his drink and stood up. 'Are you coming or not?'

'Coming where?' Ellis asked.

Hardwick smiled. 'Back to the cottage, Ellis. Back to the cottage.'

27

Again, no words were spoken as Hardwick and Flint cut through Elm Walk to head back to the cottage. Ellis had no idea what Hardwick had planned, but it still didn't seem like a good idea to him.

He was about to ask his friend whether they were going to knock on the front door or go through the back gate again when Hardwick darted across the road and up the footpath that passed behind the cottages.

Without stopping, Hardwick opened the back gate and strolled up the path. On reaching the back door, he turned briefly to make sure Ellis was with him, then pushed down on the handle. To Ellis's surprise, the door was still unlocked. He knew damn well that if he'd had two strange blokes walk into his house at night, the first thing he'd do is lock the door.

Hardwick, on the other hand, knew that the door still being unlocked probably didn't mean the occupier was lax with regards to their security. Far from it.

Hardwick let his eyes adjust to the darkness in the kitchen before stepping inside. When it became clear there was no-one in the room, he walked through into the living room.

Although he was aware of Ellis standing behind his left shoulder, he heard a heavy breath in a dark corner on the other side of the room, just before the figure of the woman appeared, brandishing a knife above her head as she charged at them.

'Hello Evelyn,' Hardwick said, standing firm and calm.

To Ellis's surprise, this seemed to defuse the situation immediately. He crawled back out from behind the sideboard and hoped no-one had heard his high-pitched squeal. He stood up and looked at the woman, who was standing, staring at Hardwick, a look of shock and sadness on her face, her greasy grey hair stuck to her forehead.

'Evelyn?' Ellis asked. 'This is Evelyn?'

Hardwick nodded slowly, not breaking eye contact with the woman.

'Yes. This is Evelyn,' Hardwick said. 'She's the—'

'That's enough,' said a familiar voice from behind them, as Rupert Pearson stood on the threshold between the kitchen and the living room. 'I think it's about time you left.'

28

After a short while, Rupert Pearson seemed to get the hint that Hardwick and Flint were going nowhere. Ellis, naturally, was quite keen to get out, but Hardwick was standing firm — and Ellis tended to go along with what his friend did.

Ellis noticed that Hardwick and Pearson had locked eyes, both waiting for the other to speak first. Unexpectedly, it was Hardwick who broke his silence first, although with good reason.

'We know what's been going on, Mr Pearson,' Hardwick said.

Ellis darted a glance at his friend, eyebrows raised.

'Well, I do, anyway. But I've no doubt Ellis would have got there eventually.' The look on Rupert Pearson's face was a combination of shock, anger and fear. 'It's

alright,' Hardwick said. 'There's no way out now. We...
I... know the truth.'

Hardwick turned towards the haggard woman.

'How long have you been doing this, Evelyn?' he
asked.

Evelyn didn't answer. The next voice that spoke was
Pearson's.

'From the beginning,' he said, before slumping into
an armchair and beginning to wail.

Hardwick looked at Flint, but said nothing. He
knew Pearson would talk. This was clearly the
moment he'd been waiting for, having kept it all
bottled up for years as the pressure built and the risks
grew too.

Eventually, Pearson's sobs subsided and he began to
calm a little.

'Evelyn is my sister,' he said, eventually. 'She's brilliant. Utterly incredible. But she can't... can't function in
normal society.'

Pearson spoke as if Evelyn wasn't still in the room.
Evelyn, on the other hand looked unperturbed by what
she was hearing. It was almost as if she wasn't hearing it
at all, but instead was in a world of her own.

'Which is why you bought this cottage for her,'
Hardwick replied.

Pearson nodded.

'But it doesn't quite explain why your wife didn't seem to know Evelyn existed.'

Pearson took a deep breath, then sighed heavily. 'It's complicated. It's just better that nobody knows. Trust me.'

'Why should nobody know?' Hardwick asked, keen to get to the truth.

Pearson locked eyes with him for a moment. His face changed slightly, giving him the look of a man resigned to his fate, with nothing left to fight for.

'It was so long ago,' he said, almost whispering. 'We were just kids.'

Hardwick nodded gently, willing him to go on.

'Evelyn had always been a troubled child,' Pearson said, smiling through tears as he looked at his sister. 'No-one quite knew how to handle her. There were constant arguments between her and my parents. They tried to control her too much, in every way. Evelyn likes boundaries, but only physically. She needs spiritual freedom. She always had.'

Pearson let out a deep sigh. 'I was sixteen when it happened. Evelyn was twenty-one. I remember hearing the argument earlier that day. Dad had told her she needed to get a job and move out. People in their twenties didn't live with their parents then. It wasn't the norm. Her peers had all flown the nest and got married.

Most had kids. But Evelyn was always a homebird. That day — that argument — Dad told her she was bloody lucky she had a home to live in at all. I can still hear his voice saying it now. The next thing I heard was her bedroom door slamming. I thought no more about it, but later that evening it all changed. Everything changed forever.'

'Go on,' Hardwick said.

Pearson swallowed hard. 'I had a girl over. Elizabeth. "Call me Lizzy" she used to say, but I hated calling her that. It was a strange house. My bedroom was next to the front door. There was a bathroom downstairs, then Evelyn's room, and upstairs was another bathroom and my parents' bedroom. My parents had gone to bed early. Dad worked shifts and was up at four in the morning. Mum did whatever Dad did. She kept to his patterns. Elizabeth and I had been in my room. I'll spare you the details. But afterwards she went to the bathroom next to my room. She was in there a while, and after a minute or so I began to smell smoke. Before I even realised what it was, I started to see it coming under the bedroom door. Like fingers, it was. Long, grey fingers. I opened my bedroom door and the hall and stairs were on fire. I could barely see a thing. Literally a minute earlier there'd been nothing, and now it was a roaring inferno.'

Pearson's voice steadied as his eyes glazed over, as if his entire self had been transported back to that evening.

'My instincts took over, and I ran out of the front door. It was already slightly open and it was as if my brain had just shut down. I didn't know what else to do but run. I remember sitting on the grass verge across the street, just watching the house burn. I couldn't do anything. I couldn't move, couldn't speak. And that's when I saw Evelyn. She was a little further up the lane, sitting under a tree, watching the same thing I was but with a blank look on her face. I knew then what had happened. Who had started the fire.

'People were coming up to me. Someone said they'd called the fire brigade. I couldn't speak. Couldn't do anything. I just sat there, looking at the house. Later, they told me they'd found three bodies in the house. Two in the upstairs bedroom and a young woman in the downstairs bathroom. They'd been so badly burned there were just fragments of bones left. They only knew it was a young woman downstairs because her pelvis had been left mostly intact. One of the neighbours told the fire brigade that Mum, Dad, Evelyn and I lived there. They just assumed that the young woman in the downstairs bathroom had been Evelyn. Things were done differently back then. It all just... it was skimmed over so quickly. From that point on, Evelyn was officially dead.'

'Although she was still very much alive,' Hardwick said.

'Yes. I was offered help. Told I could stay with relatives. But I turned it all down. I lived in a bedsit for nearly two years while I saved up enough money to buy my own place. There was a bit of money from my parents, but that didn't go very far. And the house wasn't insured. The police didn't even suspect me. Not that I expected them to, of course, but it was only months later that I realised I would have been the prime suspect. Maybe they could see something. Maybe it was the level of shock I was in. I guess I'll never know.'

'What happened to Elizabeth?' Ellis asked, his voice rasping.

Pearson drew a deep breath before letting it out as a long, drawn-out sigh.

'She was reported missing. By her family. They didn't know about me. No-one did. Her parents were odd, religious types. She was only allowed out of the house because she told them she was going to the church's youth club. I just... kept quiet. If it had happened maybe a week or two later, perhaps someone would have known about us and the link would've been made. But they didn't. And it wasn't. I don't know when it all ended. At first there were searches and door-to-door enquiries and then... then it just sort of fizzled out without anyone ever really noticing.

'I used to go back to the house every week. Where the house had been, I mean. One week, Evelyn was there, sitting under that same tree. I can't explain how I felt, but it was as if I really had believed she was dead and that seeing her again was as if she'd come back to life. I mean, I knew Elizabeth had died and Evelyn hadn't, but perhaps it was just my brain trying to make sense of it all. I suppose nowadays it'd be called PTSD. I walked over and sat down next to her. We both just sat in silence for what seemed like hours, staring at the burnt-out shell that had been our family home. It sounds bizarre, but I didn't feel anything. I should have been angry, out of my mind, sitting next to the sister who'd murdered our parents and my girlfriend. But there was nothing.

'After a while I started to visit less frequently. Maybe just birthdays, Christmasses and anniversaries. And then not at all. I don't know when I stopped, or which was my last visit. But Evelyn still managed to find me. It was seven years after the fire. I received a letter, from Evelyn. I don't remember what it said. I was just captivated by her beautiful handwriting and the flow of her words. It was like reading poetry.'

Pearson stopped talking, the rheumy look in his eyes

quickly disappearing as he snapped back into the present.

'And that's why Cathy's never heard about Evelyn,' he said, as if that would put the whole matter to bed.

'But there's a reason why you still keep a roof over her head, isn't there?' Hardwick asked, his eyes slowly moving across the room to the stack of papers on the coffee table.

Pearson looked back at Hardwick, his eyes cold and steely.

'I think it's time you left now.'

Hardwick shook his head slowly. 'No, I think it's time you told us the whole truth.'

29

By now, Evelyn was rocking in the corner of the room, clearly deeply disturbed by events and the resurgence of past feelings.

'Can't you see what this is doing to her?' Pearson barked.

'I can indeed,' Hardwick replied. 'Although I really don't see how Ellis or I can be blamed for it. How about we perk her up a bit, hmmm? Why don't you tell us more about your sister, the troubled genius?'

Pearson pursed his lips, knowing full well where Hardwick was going with this.

'Your sister isn't just a wonderful writer of letters, is she? She's also a wonderful writer of books.'

Pearson's eyes narrowed, and in that moment he looked as if he wanted to kill Hardwick.

'You see, Mr Pearson, it's all started to become rather clear. There's a reason you don't do readings from your own novels, isn't there? Not only do you *not* write your own novels, but you *can't* write them. Or read them. Can you? And that's why Veronica Campbell used to do the readings at your book launches. It's also why you had a policy of never signing books. Because what if someone wanted a personalised dedication? You couldn't very well say no, could you?

'When we turned up at your house and asked you about Aspire Creative Solutions, I showed you a document from Companies House. Except I'd doctored the document and switched most of the letters around. You didn't even notice. You can't write and you can barely read, can you?'

Pearson's eyes were still locked on to Hardwick's, but he continued.

'Which is why your sister, Evelyn, wrote every single word of every novel that carries your name. And that's why, when Veronica Campbell discovered the truth, you knew you had to kill her.'

Ellis leaned in towards Hardwick. 'Kempston, he couldn't have done. He was at the pub with us at the time Veronica died.'

'Was he, though?' Hardwick asked.

'I didn't get on well at school,' Rupert said, ignoring

their comments. 'Barely ever went in. In the end, they threw me out. I got in with the wrong crowd. The worse I did, the better Evelyn got. The better she did, the worse I got. We were like magnets pointing in opposite directions. She was the overachiever, I was the waster. I even tried turning my hand to learning when I was older, but I couldn't. Words and letters just jump about all over the place. It's impossible. Nowadays, they'd diagnose severe dyslexia, but back then I was just thick. There was no support. Everything I know I've learned from television, radio and audiobooks.'

Ellis was still uneasy. 'Kempston, he was literally standing in front of us when Veronica died. He didn't do it.'

Kempston raised his index finger. 'We know he was at the pub with us at the time showing on Veronica's smashed watch. Do you have a watch Ellis?'

Ellis lifted his sleeve to show Hardwick his watch.

'Me too,' Hardwick said. I don't know about you, but I'm forever bashing mine on things. Doorframes, mostly. At least twice a day. The tempered glass faces are pretty strong, don't you think? For how often we scratch or hit the face of our watches on things, they almost never even leave the slightest mark — let alone smash into smithereens. Although if someone were to deliberately break the watch and set the time to show — oh, I don't know, let's say ten past nine — one might reasonably assume that was the time the wearer was attacked and died. Of course, forensic pathologists can only give a very rough window during which death occurred. They're often out by hours — let alone the few minutes it would take to get from Tollinghill Country Park to the Freemason's Arms.

'And that's what you did, isn't it?' Hardwick said, staring into Rupert Pearson's eyes. 'You killed Veronica, broke her watch, turned the hands to ten past nine — knowing full well you'd be at your own book launch with dozens of witnesses before then — and headed for the warm comfort of the Freemason's Arms. Tell me, Mr Pearson. How long has Evelyn lived here in this cottage, writing your novels for you?'

Pearson blinked once. 'Since the beginning. Thirty-eight years.'

Hardwick nodded slowly. 'And how many times in thirty-eight years has she left the cottage?'

Pearson took a deep breath and lifted his chin. 'Never.'

'Thirty-eight years. Almost four decades in the same building. Incarcerated. The same way she'd have been incarcerated if she'd been convicted of three murders.'

Hardwick loosened his shoulders and sighed. 'So. Do you want to call the police or shall I?'

In that moment, Pearson's demeanour changed. His hands went into his jacket pockets and came back out again, one holding a kitchen knife and the other a cigarette lighter.

'History has a funny way of repeating itself, doesn't it?' he said, pointing the knife at Hardwick and Flint. 'A mysterious fire, three people die. Something poetic about it, don't you think?' Pearson started laughing. 'I might use it for inspiration for my next novel. Oh wait!'

'Forensic fire investigation is a lot more advanced than it was back then, I can assure you,' Hardwick said. 'They'll probably be able to tell exactly what brand of lighter was used. Not to mention the fact that CCTV will have tracked you on your way here.'

'CCTV? At this end of Tollinghill? Don't make me laugh,' Pearson said. 'And anyway, why should I care? I've got nothing left to lose. If you get out of here in one piece, my life's over. At least this way I've got a chance.'

Hardwick shook his head. 'I'm afraid not. Although your life might have been a series of lucky — and unlucky — events, I plan everything assiduously. Detective Inspector?'

Pearson turned just in time to see DI Warner and his colleague, Detective Constable Sam Kerrigan, appear from the kitchen, immediately disarming and hand-cuffing him.

30

It wasn't something most people ever got to experience, but the atmosphere after unmasking a killer was different to that beforehand. It was almost as if a fog had lifted; as if the windows had been black, but were now letting light in.

The windows hadn't seemed black before, nor was the fog visible, and it was only now the ordeal was largely over that the previous state had become apparent.

But, somehow, the Freemason's Arms seemed warmer, more inviting. More welcoming. At least, as welcoming as it could ever be with Doug Lilley at the helm.

'What, so he bumped her off then legged it over here for his book launch?' the landlord said, disbelief clear in his voice, after Ellis had finished regaling him with the outcome of their investigation.

'That's about the sum of it, yes,' Hardwick replied.

'Cheeky blighter. I must say, I'm not at all happy about people committing murders then coming into my pub. That's the sort of thing that gets a place a bad name.'

'Yes, well I'm not sure it'll become a regular occurrence.'

'I should hope not. That's two now, in eight years.'

'I wonder what the average number of murders in a pub is,' Ellis said, far too seriously, turning towards Hardwick. 'Do you think it's more or less than two in eight years?'

Hardwick blinked a few times. 'I must say it's not something I've ever really sat down and analysed, but I should wholeheartedly imagine it's significantly less than two.'

'One then?'

'Well, no. I'd say even that's too many,' Hardwick explained.

'But people do get murdered in pubs, don't they?'

'Yes. It has been known.'

'And you can't have, say, half a murder, can you? Or point two nine of a murder?'

'Physically speaking, no, but statistics are—'

'Well there you go then,' Ellis said, as if that settled the matter.

Hardwick, not relishing trying to explain the basics of statistics to Ellis, forced a smile and changed the subject.

'In any case,' he said, turning to Doug, 'I think it's safe to say that Rupert Pearson won't be holding any more book launches in your pub any time soon.'

'Well, that's one night every year or two I'm going to have to fill with something else. Maybe we can hold a Lunar Eclipse Night.'

'Never heard of those,' Ellis said. 'Must be a Fettlesham thing.'

'I'm pretty stunned DI Warner believed you,' Doug said, also now ignoring Ellis.

Hardwick shuffled slightly. 'I think even Detective Inspector Warner has a point where he has to admit he was wrong. As much as it might pain him to say it.'

'I dunno. I still reckon it was that Terry. Seemed like a wrong'un to me.'

As if on cue, the front door of the Freemason's Arms opened and Detective Inspector Rob Warner walked in.

'Hardwick.'

'Detective Inspector.'

'I thought you might like a drink.'

'Did you?'

'The CPS have authorised a charge on Pearson.'

'Already?'

'Pretty cut and dried. He coughed. Told us the lot. We found traces of blood in the boot of his car, where he'd dumped his clothes after killing her. Unfortunately for him, he kept the clothes he was wearing when he killed her, and there were traces of blood on those too. It came back as a match to Veronica. Bet he wishes he'd got a new washing machine now.'

'And what about his sister, Evelyn?'

Warner shrugged. 'None of our concern. She's a grown adult. There were talks about investigating the death of her parents all those years ago, but there didn't seem a whole lot of point. What good would it do?'

'It might get her some psychiatric help.'

'That's what we thought, but she passed the psych assessments with flying colours. That means one of two things. Either she wasn't mad after all — which I find hard to believe after spending however many years locked up in that cottage — or she's completely stark raving bonkers but underneath it all she's so cunning and smart that she managed to fool the psychiatric experts.'

Hardwick thought for a moment, rather uneasy at the possibility that Evelyn had not been quite as abused and downtrodden as had been made out, but actually had quite a lot of control over the situation.

'What about the books?' he asked. 'And the estate. What happens to that if he's in prison?'

'Pearson made noises about signing over the intellectual property rights to her, but we'll see how that pans out. The money won't be much use to him where he's going.'

'I imagine it won't be insignificant either,' Hardwick said. 'I should think The Clarion Call will hit the top of the bestseller lists this week. The Great British public loves nothing more than a scandal.'

'No such luck. The publishers have pulled all unsold copies from the shelves. Not sure if that was a smart move or not, if you ask me. The ones that are left out there will be massive collectors' items. Here, I hope you held on to your copy.'

'Certainly not.'

Warner chuckled to himself. 'I did. I had DC Kerrigan pop out and clear the shelves at WH Smith's before the news broke. I've got sixteen copies sitting at home in my living room. We're in the money!' Warner began, breaking into song.

Hardwick smiled graciously and let his eyes fall on the presentation box of limited edition whisky sitting proudly on the shelf behind the bar.

'Very good, Detective Inspector. Now, about that drink...'

The woman browsed the shelves and racks of the charity shop with a soft smile on her face. It wasn't the grin of someone who was deliriously happy or even thinking about anything in particular — just the gentle resting smile of someone who was, finally, content.

She let her eyes fall across the bookshelves, taking in the names and titles of all of these beautiful books. Pre-owned, pre-read, pre-loved. She liked those terms. They implied that the real ownership, real reading and real love was yet to come.

Eventually, her eyes settled on one particular tome. Now that she noticed it, it stood out like a sore thumb. She pulled the title from the bookshelf and stroked the cover gently.

She turned the book over and read the blurb on the

back. It didn't sound like much, but it had a certain appeal. She might never read it, but that was okay. She had plenty of books she had never read and probably would never read.

She carried the book over to the counter and placed it down, smiling at the elderly woman behind the till.

'Will that be all, love?'

'Yes, thank you.'

The shop worker's eyes widened as she registered the item the woman was buying.'

'Oh, The Clarion Call. Rupert Pearson. Local author, he is. Rumour has it this book might be worth a bit of money. Do you know the story behind it? Did you hear what he did?'

'Yes,' the woman said, gently. 'Yes, I heard.'

The older woman looked at her and smiled. 'That'll be two pounds eighty, please, love.'

She handed over her money and took the book, placing it in the inside pocket of her large winter coat, before saying goodbye.

The shop worker watched as her customer headed for the exit, her lank grey hair sticking to her head as she opened the door and disappeared onto the streets of Tollinghill.

# GET MORE OF MY BOOKS FREE!

Thank you for reading *The Wrong Man*. I hope it was as much fun for you as it was for me writing it.

**To say thank you, I'd like to invite you to my exclusive *VIP Club*, and give you some of my books and short stories for FREE. All members of my VIP Club have access to FREE, exclusive books and short stories which aren't available anywhere else.**

**You'll also get access to all of my new releases at a bargain-basement price before they're available anywhere else. Joining is absolutely FREE and you can leave at any time, no questions asked. To join the club,**

**head to** adamcroft.net/vip-club **and two free books will be sent to you straight away!**

If you enjoyed the book, please do leave a review on the site you bought it from. Reviews mean an awful lot to writers and they help us to find new readers more than almost anything else. It would be very much appreciated.

I love hearing from my readers, too, so please do feel free to get in touch with me. You can contact me via my website, on Twitter @adamcroft and you can 'like' my Facebook page at facebook.com/adamcroftbooks.

**For more information, visit my website:** adamcroft.net

.

Printed in Great Britain
by Amazon